CHAPTER ONE

Wedding

Libby Forest dropped into a wooden chair, exhausted. She'd spent the afternoon on tenterhooks, half-expecting an unforeseen disaster to ruin the wedding, but the ceremony had passed without a hitch. Now, in a sturdy marquee pitched in a field, the reception was underway. The level of excited chatter rose as guests finished their meals, nibbling cheddar cheese and biscuits, their stomachs full of Somerset beef and local apple pie. The temptation to giggle grew until it was almost irresistible and Libby had to turn it into a sneeze.

Max Ramshore, even more handsome than usual, squeezed her hand. "Are you coming down with a cold? Or is it an attack of maternal emotion at seeing your son marry?"

"Neither. It's pure relief. I can hardly believe the wedding's over and everything went well. I've been expecting the worst all day."

"Don't count your chickens. Remember what happened at the Oscars. Nothing's over until it finishes."

"That sounds very cryptic," Libby said, "but at least Bear was on his best behaviour." Libby let her fingers sink into the warm fur of the huge Carpathian sheepdog by her side. "He didn't smell the cathedral cat and chase him down the aisle. He thinks cats exist on this earth for his personal entertainment. I hope no one's planned any practical jokes."

"Don't look at me. I've never found old tin cans tied to cars especially amusing."

Libby took a moment to gaze round the marquee. The happy couple looked radiant, the service had been touching, and old friends of the bride's family had filled the cathedral. Libby, still new to Somerset, had fewer guests to invite, but the sight of a row of customers from the bakery in the congregation had lifted her heart. Even Mrs Marchant, the old lady who collected stray cats from the streets of Wells, had attended, her dress so old and lace-covered it surely counted as vintage.

Libby shot a glance at Mandy, her apprentice. Dressed in full Gothic splendour, including a tight black bodice and voluminous skirt, Mandy sat beside Reginald, Max's basketball-playing American colleague. Libby recognised Steve, Mandy's ex-boyfriend, at the same table. She winced. Would he cause a scene?

Max wagged his finger. "Stop worrying about Mandy."

Libby wriggled. "Did you talk to Reginald? You know, about being too old for her?"

"I most certainly did not. I thought we'd agreed she's an adult and can look after herself. She's having a ball with both her admirers in attendance. From the way Steve's looking at her, all big brown puppy eyes, I think he's hoping to get her back. They only broke up because she wouldn't visit him in London."

"*Couldn't* visit," Libby corrected. "She still has a phobia that stops her travelling by train."

"Well, maybe she could get some help. There are therapists, you know. Anyway, it's not your responsibility. Just relax for once and enjoy your son's wedding reception. The marquee's full of people you don't know, any one of whom may be plotting murder. Look." He nodded towards a small huddle of Robert's friends. "Do you think one of those might be a candidate?"

"Don't even think it. I want a perfect day today, with no crises."

Max wandered away, seeking out old friends, while Libby breathed a happy sigh, slipped her feet out of new, painfully high heels, and watched Sarah's mother approach. Belinda looked beautiful and voluptuous as always. In a powder blue jacket, navy shoes and wide brimmed hat, she would be every inch the serene mother of the bride, were it not for the tense lines on her forehead and the occasional anxious glance to left and right.

She sank into the chair next to Libby. "I know this isn't the time…"

Libby suppressed a groan as she recognised the tone of voice. Belinda had a favour to ask. Libby's fame as an investigator had grown locally, and she was approached in the most inappropriate places. At least Belinda hadn't followed her into the ladies.

"How can I help?"

Sarah's mother licked her lips and hesitated. Libby nodded towards Sarah. "Your daughter looks beautiful; the perfect bride."

"The thing is…" Belinda swallowed and picked at the skin of her thumb.

Libby took pity. "Why don't we have a cup of tea? Sarah and Robert are still circulating, so we've got time for a chat."

Belinda visibly relaxed. "It's a bit embarrassing. Confidential. I need to know you'll be discreet." A hint of steel underpinned the words.

"Of course."

"It's about money, I'm afraid."

Libby hid a smile. Aside from marital problems, financial embarrassments were the most common reason people asked for private investigations. "Before you begin, is this an official request or are you asking as a friend?"

Belinda seemed taken aback. "Oh, I suppose it's official." She'd probably been hoping for free professional advice, but experience had taught Libby it was best to establish from the outset that a formal private investigation carried a price tag.

The bride's mother coughed and fiddled with an earring as she recovered her dignity. "I just need to recoup some money. I had a small legacy when my mother died a couple of years ago. I invested it, but the—er—the shares collapsed and I made a loss." She bit her lower lip. "I promised Sarah help with the wedding expenses. We don't have much spare cash in the farm, what with the milk prices over the past year, so I didn't want to worry Sarah's dad about it, but soon I'm going to have to stump up the money."

Libby offered a sympathetic smile, secretly intrigued. It was obvious Belinda was only telling half the story. Did she suspect she'd been cheated? Or perhaps she'd done something foolish. Had she been borrowing money from loan sharks?

Libby glanced over her shoulder. This wasn't a good place for further confidences. "I'll need as much detail as possible. Perhaps we could meet tomorrow and go through your accounts?"

Belinda chewed harder on her lip. Libby waited, giving her time. Max, her business partner, would be able to help with the woman's financial problems. Until recently, he'd worked for the government on international fraud and money laundering. He could sort out poor accounting and advise on improved budgeting and wealth management, but Libby suspected Belinda's problems extended further.

"It's a bit complicated…" Belinda's voice wavered as a man wearing a grey linen kaftan approached. Tall and striking, he stood out among the other guests, who mostly wore more conventional wedding clothes. Long grey hair was drawn back into a ponytail, and the man's bushy grey eyebrows framed a strong face characterised by sharp cheekbones and a hooked nose. Belinda stiffened as he approached.

He smiled, but his light grey eyes peered intensely into her face. "Belinda, my dear. I haven't seen you for a while. Thank you so much for the invitation to your daughter's wedding, but I'm afraid my wife sends her apologies. Her mother is unwell. Nothing serious, but the old lady has a heavy cold and Olivia felt she shouldn't be left alone."

His words were commonplace, but the man's effect on Belinda was electric. She jumped to her feet, cheeks reddening. "It's a-a pleasure, Sandy." In the awkward pause that followed, Libby slipped her feet back into her shoes, stepped forward, and held out a hand. With a little start, as though recollecting her manners, Belinda said, "Let me introduce Xavier Papadopoulos. He's a sort of distant cousin of mine."

"And you're the mother of our handsome groom, Mrs Forest." He pronounced the name slowly, rolling it round his mouth as though tasting each syllable.

The back of Libby's neck prickled with discomfort. "We're delighted Robert found Sarah. She's a lovely young woman."

Unblinking, the man watched her face, his smile enigmatic. "Indeed." After an unnerving pause, he seemed to lose interest. The snake-like eyes re-focused on Belinda. "I'm sure we'll have plenty of time to talk this evening, while the young people dance, Belinda."

She cleared her throat. "I-I'll look forward to it." The lie was obvious.

Without another word the grey man left. He strolled through the marquee with slow, measured steps, his back ramrod straight. Heads turned as he passed, as though his personal magnetism sucked in everyone within range. Libby breathed out, suddenly tired. "Your cousin's a most unusual person."

Belinda's head turned towards Libby, but her eyes were vague. "I'm sorry. What did you say?"

Maybe she didn't want to discuss the man. Instead, Libby made a suggestion. "Would you like an appointment? I'll ask Max to come. He'll help with your money worries. He's something of a financial genius, and very discreet."

Belinda let out a little gasp, grabbed her bag, and hurried towards the exit. "N-no thanks. Forget I said anything. It's nothing really. I'll talk to Mike and we'll sort things out." She threw the words over her shoulder a she hurried away.

Libby's mind seethed with curiosity. Why had the arrival of Xavier Papadopoulos upset Belinda so? Was it just that she was worried about being overheard?

Libby doubted that was the reason for the woman's change of heart. Instinct told her Belinda was frightened of Xavier Papadopoulos.

Next moment, she'd forgotten about Belinda Carmichael. The atmosphere in the marquee had changed, the gentle hubbub of cheerful conversation died away. Libby rose, confused, as an angry voice carried from the far end of the marquee. Libby couldn't make out the words.

Then, her son Robert was at Libby's side. "Sarah's aunt's causing an almighty fuss. She's saying her ring's been stolen. Can you come and help sort it out?"

Libby closed her eyes. Everything had been going too smoothly. She'd known something would go wrong.

CHAPTER TWO

Lady Antonia

Like a ship in full sail, a regal figure in lilac satin bore down on the group of three, wearing a hat apparently constructed entirely of pearls. Libby recognised Lady Antonia Appleby, the widow of Sir John Appleby, one of Somerset's wealthiest farmers. Lady Antonia drew near, face purple, chin vibrating. "No one's leaving until my ring's been found."

"One of these *people…*" She spat the word as though swearing, one arm sweeping in a wide gesture that encompassed everyone in the marquee. Ears strained to catch every word of this new entertainment. "One of these guests has stolen a valuable family heirloom and I insist the police are called immediately."

Sarah, face pale and pinched, took her great aunt's arm. "Aunt Antonia, there's no need for that. You must have dropped the ring somewhere. It won't take long for us to find it."

"Nonsense," the woman barked. "I don't drop

things. I pride myself on taking care of my possessions. When you have responsibilities like mine, you learn to pay attention to the things that matter. Now, are you going to call the police, or shall I?"

"Please, wait a moment," Sarah sounded desperate. "This is Mrs Forest. She's a private investigator—"

The woman interrupted. "I'm not interested in some kind of amateur sleuth. My diamond ring is worth thousands of pounds and I insist on calling in the professionals."

Max, who'd been chatting with friends outside the tent, strolled inside, his smile relaxed as though he remained entirely unaware of any tension in the air. "Why, Lady Antonia." He turned the full force of his blue eyes on her, and Libby felt a small jolt of pride as he took control of the situation. "I hadn't seen you here. I wonder if I can help."

"Maxwell Ramshore. It's been a long time since we met. I don't believe you've visited for years. Not since my old friend, your mother, died."

"My loss."

Libby was constantly meeting friends and acquaintances of Max, from all walks of life. Women seemed to melt when they saw him. Libby tried not to be jealous. After all, it was his easy charm that had first attracted her to him. More importantly, though, she'd soon learned to recognise and admire the steel that underpinned his warm smile and Scandinavian blue eyes.

Max took Antonia Appleby's arm, conjured a comfortable chair from nowhere, and within seconds had seated her in front of a tall glass of champagne. Libby joined them and Max shot a quick glance at her face, followed by the faintest wink. "Now, Lady Antonia. Tell me about your missing ring. Is it that beautiful diamond cluster I remember you wearing at some of those parties you used to throw? My, those were some evenings."

The woman nodded and tossed back half a glass of champagne. Perhaps her purple face was not due solely to fury at losing a ring. Several previous glasses of champagne were probably to blame. She beamed at Max. "Ah, those were the days, when my husband was alive. We used to dance until dawn, and if I remember correctly, you were one of the most eligible bachelors in the room. You and poor William."

Max murmured in Libby's ear, "William was their son. He was a merchant banker when I started at my first firm, but he joined the army and died in Bosnia."

Lady Antonia was still talking. "When William was a little boy, he used to love that ring. He would make me take it from the safe and let the sun shine through it so he could see rainbows." Emotion glinted in her eyes.

Max touched her hand. "I can tell your ring's very precious. Let's see if we can't track it down. First, I think we should make sure it isn't in your bag." He held up a finger, forestalling any objections. "I know, we won't find it there, but the police would insist. After all, it could have slipped off your finger when you reached for a handkerchief or pulled out some confetti…"

Mollified, Antonia Appleby clicked open her bag and emptied the contents in a small heap on the pristine white tablecloth. Handkerchief, comb, lipstick, and powder compact, the indispensable accompaniment to a formal occasion for a woman like Lady Antonia. She opened a small silver case and held it out for Max to see. "See, there's William in his uniform with his father. Both of them gone, now."

Libby leaned across to catch a glimpse of a tall, tanned man in the uniform of the Coldstream Guards, his arm around an older man. Both men shared similar Roman noses, but the older of the two had an impressive shock of white hair and wore a mayoral chain around his neck. Libby swallowed the lump that had formed in her throat and forgave the lonely widow her need for alcohol.

"Nothing there. I told you so." Lady Antonia snatched up the handkerchief and touched one corner delicately to her eyes.

Max helped replace the items in her bag. "Indeed you did. Now, why don't you talk to my business partner, Libby Forest. She works miracles, finding missing treasures." Max's gaze met Libby's. The last thing Libby had retrieved was a missing cat, but there was no need to tell Lady Antonia. "If she can't find your ring, of course we'll call the police."

"Isn't your son, a what-do-you-call-it? Locks people up? A policeman, that's the word. Don't suppose he's of sufficiently high rank to lead an important investigation like this."

"Joe's recently been promoted. He's a detective inspector, now." Max spoke casually, but there was no mistaking the pride in his voice.

"In that case," Lady Antonia pronounced, "I can't think of anyone better to help, if necessary. Still, I'll let this young lady try first. Ask me your questions." She pushed her face close to Libby's. "Let's see what you're made of."

Confused by the elderly lady's sudden mood changes, but happy to be called young, for once, Libby asked, "I believe you're Sarah's aunt?"

"Exactly so. Great aunt. No, aunt." The woman frowned, waved a hand in the air, and took another gulp of wine. "Something like that."

"What time did you arrive at the cathedral?"

"I was one of the first. It gave me the opportunity to catch up with the man in charge. Wearing one of those red robes. Family friend, you see. We had a good old chat. What was his name, now?" She frowned, but after a moment her brow cleared. "Oh, never mind. Now, where was I?"

Was Lady Antonia's difficulty with names just due to the wine, or was there a problem? Libby couldn't tell. With care, she led the old lady through the details of the wedding day. It turned out Lady Antonia always travelled by taxi. "Did you have the ring on your finger when you arrived at the cathedral?"

"Cathedral? What cathedral? I haven't set foot in the place since they refused to let me bury my husband in the crypt. Ridiculous rules and regulations. A man of my husband's importance should rest in the most prominent position, don't you know?"

She peered at Libby. "What was I saying? Oh, yes. I talked to the rector at the church."

Libby let the confusion pass. It hardly mattered if the old lady thought Wells Cathedral was just a church. "When you arrived here, at the farm, you were wearing the ring?"

"I especially remember because I saw several of the local people glancing at it. I only remove it from the bank for special occasions. Weddings and funerals." She pointed at Sarah, who was watching proceedings from a distance. "She's wearing my family pearls, today."

"Something borrowed," Libby acknowledged. "I expect you were looking forward to a family celebration."

The woman drained the remainder of her champagne and Max replaced it with a full glass. "I felt an obligation to represent my side of the family, although a wedding reception on farmland seems a little…" Lady Antonia surveyed the marquee from one end to another, "A little *unusual.*"

With every word, Libby grew more convinced the poor woman was struggling with memory problems. It complicated matters. Had she really been wearing the ring, or had she left it at home? There was no way to tell, unless someone had noticed it on her finger. Perhaps Sarah had seen it.

Leaving Max to entertain his mother's old friend, Libby joined the newly-wed couple for a whispered conversation. Sarah confirmed her great aunt had frequent memory lapses. "I don't remember seeing the ring today, but she would usually wear it. It's her pride and joy, because

Uncle Humphrey bought it for their first wedding anniversary. She's lost a lot of weight recently. I don't think she eats properly, now she's living alone. The ring was loose and it could easily have slipped from her finger."

"Could we organise a quick search, in case she just dropped it?"

Robert's eyes sparkled at the idea of gathering their friends, boisterous with champagne, to scour the surroundings. "Like a treasure hunt."

Max had overheard. "I'm sure they'll find it. I'd lay odds the ring just slipped off her finger."

After an hour, though, Robert and Sarah admitted defeat. The ring was nowhere to be found.

***

"Time to call in the police?" Max suggested.

Lady Antonia's enthusiasm for the local constabulary had waned. "Perhaps we should leave it until tomorrow." Her words slurred together. "We don't want to spoil the wedding."

Libby hunted for Belinda, finally locating her outside the marquee, well away from her aunt. "Is it the alcohol talking, or is Lady Antonia really having second thoughts about calling the police? Do you know how much the ring's really worth?"

17

Belinda concentrated on the nail she was nibbling, despite ruining an expensive wedding manicure. "I think she likes the attention. She's very old and forgetful. Why don't you leave her to me and I'll talk to her tomorrow? After all, we don't want to make a fuss." With a little wave of her fingers, she disappeared into the melee of wedding guests.

"I don't know what to make of it," Libby confessed to Max. "One minute, Belinda has a problem she wants me to solve and her aunt's ring is so valuable we need the police. Then, it turns out both problems were no more than silly mistakes. I'm beginning to think Sarah's mother and great aunt have more in common than first appears."

"Both got loose screws, you mean?"

"Hope not. My son's married into that family, don't forget."

Max gave an exaggerated groan. "Have you thought about the grandchildren? How are they going to turn out?" Libby just rolled her eyes as he went on, "What about this missing ring?"

"Just thank our lucky stars Lady Antonia hasn't insisted on the police. She can claim the insurance if it doesn't turn up."

They walked outside, enjoying the smell of newly mown hay, and the tang of dairy cows, lying in the quiet summer air. "It's been a strange afternoon."

"I love the way mystery follows you around." Max linked his arm with Libby's. "If you're worried, we could do a little quiet sleuthing to see what's worrying Belinda. What do you know about the rest of the family?"

"There's Sarah's father, Mike. According to Sarah, he spends every waking hour out in the fields or in his office managing the farm."

"I don't know Mike well," Max said. "But he's a member of the skittles team."

Libby laughed. "That's a vote of confidence, then."

"Who's that talking to Sarah?"

"Tim. He's Sarah's older brother, but doesn't live on the farm. Works for a feed company in Minehead, I believe."

It was almost dark, the clear sky filling with stars. "Time for the evening entertainment?" Max took Libby's arm as they strolled inside to find a group of young farmers clutching guitars, ukuleles, and an accordion.

The leader counted, "One, two, three, four…" the guests cheered, and the band launched into one of the Wurzels' greatest hits.

As the quests roared out a chorus at the top of their lungs, the marquee shuddered and rocked as a heavy weight hit the canvas. A woman screamed. After a moment of stunned silence, the guests rushed outside to find a young man entangled in guy ropes.

He staggered up, cursing. Sarah's brother Tim, smart wedding suit tight on the legs and arms, fists raised, aimed a punch at the young man's head. "I know you took it."

This time, his opponent was ready. He ducked sideways and Tim crashed to the ground. Winded, he gasped, "Search his pockets. He's got the ring."

"You lying…"

Robert appeared. "What's going on? Tim, what's this all about?"

"Liam Weston's got the ring. I saw him pick it up." Tim stood, brushing grass from his jacket.

The other lad narrowed his eyes. Built like a boxer, he looked capable of giving Tim Carmichael a hammering. "I dropped a coin, that's all."

"Prove it."

Sarah was sobbing. "Tim, please don't do this. You've had too much to drink."

"Look here, Sarah." Liam Weston held out his hands. "You know I'd never steal from your family. You've known me all your life."

Sarah gulped.

"Tell you what, I'll turn my pockets out. Prove

my innocence."

He handed his jacket to Sarah. "Look in the pockets."

Sarah slid her hand into each pocket, one after another, inside and out. "There's nothing there." She held out one hand, showing the stub of a pencil and a few coins. "That's all he's got."

Tim's mouth twisted. "What about his trouser pockets?"

"Oh, really." Sarah snapped. "You're going too far."

Tim thrust his hands into the pockets of Liam's trousers and, with a triumphant flourish, held up the ring. "See. Here it is."

CHAPTER THREE

Bridge

"A dose of fresh air is just what we need." Max turned off the Land Rover's engine and opened all the doors. Bear leapt out and waited, tongue lolling, for Shipley to follow. "Should we keep Shipley on the lead?"

Libby came round the car and leaned against the door, breathing in the scent of summer on Exmoor. "I think we should. He's only lived with you a few days. He's always been a bit wild, and he's hard to control when he's over-excited. I wouldn't trust him around sheep."

Libby had walked Shipley for his former owner when she first arrived in Exham on Sea. It broke her heart when he was abandoned. Tanya, the local vet, had taken him in on a temporary basis, but Libby begged Max to take him on as a companion to Bear. She wondered if she'd made a mistake. Shipley was a springer spaniel, a breed known for excitability. He'd chased her cat, Fuzzy, into hiding in the airing cupboard on his first visit.

A warm breeze whipped Libby's hair against her face. "That was some wedding reception."

"I used to think my job was exciting until you came to Exham."

Libby giggled. "The past two years have been like a roller-coaster. I never know what's going to happen next. Good job I like surprises. It was a funny day, yesterday. I mean, apart from that stupid fight. Watching my only son get married made me feel old…" Her voice died away. She avoided mentioning marriage when she was with Max. He'd made it plain he wanted Libby in his life, and he'd mentioned marriage, but he'd never asked in so many words if she would be his wife. She was glad of that, for she found it impossible to decide how she'd answer. Marriage seemed so final.

Libby's friend, Angela, had suggested Max was scared she might turn him down, but Libby had snorted. The man was so confident, so self-assured. If he wanted something, he'd ask for it. Angela had raised an immaculate eyebrow and given a knowing smile. "People put on a good front, sometimes, to avoid disappointment. Is Max really as confident as you imagine? Maybe his divorce put him off another wedding."

Libby grimaced. Her own marriage hadn't worked so well the first time, with Trevor. Her law-abiding, insurance agent husband had turned out to be a criminal. If he hadn't died suddenly, he'd probably be in prison right now. As a result, reluctant to make another mistake, she'd reached some kind of impasse with Max. They'd agreed they wanted a relationship, but each kept stepping back from the brink of marriage.

As though following her train of thought, a discomforting knack he possessed, Max asked, "Have Robert and Ali recovered from the shock of finding their father was a crook?"

"Ali's seeking solace in fixing the world's problems. She's still in Brazil, volunteering. Robert was close to Trevor, but now he has Sarah." Libby tugged Shipley's lead, pulling him back from Bear, who'd tracked down an interesting scent. "I've recovered, too, mainly thanks to you, Max."

"Stop. You'll make me blush." As Max laughed, Libby breathed more easily. She'd navigated the awkward moment in safety.

They followed a path through a field. Nearby, the hedges rustled with life. The air was filled with the song of blue tits and wrens, and from time to time a sparrow flashed across the path, driving Shipley mad with frustration. Dunster Castle dominated a hill in the distance. By the side of the field trickled one of the rivers that criss-cross Exmoor, its banks wooded with oak and beech. A lark rose, singing its heart-lifting song. Libby stopped and shaded her eyes against the sun, trying to spot the bird as it spiralled high in the air. "Bear. Come here." Bear looked over his shoulder, hesitated, finally lumbering back to her side. "Should we find out more about the ring, do you think?"

Max snorted. "I was waiting for you to suggest it—I knew you couldn't resist the temptation. Of course, we won't get paid—not that you ever charge enough."

Libby winced. She'd been a successful baker and chocolatier, but the fledgling private investigation service posed a far greater financial challenge. She often undertook inquiries for nothing.

"The really interesting cases are too exciting to resist, even when no one's paying for our services. Like the body in the cathedral library…"

Max threw a stick for Bear. "I'm glad you said that, because you're right. It's hard to make ends meet on an ad hoc basis. I've been doing a few calculations of my own, and after a lot of negotiation, I've agreed an arrangement with my previous employers."

"The government. You mean, you haven't entirely given up spying?"

He laughed. "I think describing my financial

audits as spying is going a bit far. Still, I heard from the police head honcho the other day. I did some work with them, if you remember, over a ring of vehicle thieves. The Chief Constable is looking at some kind of consultancy, paying a retainer, so he can call on private investigation services at short notice."

Libby fell silent.

"What's wrong?" Max frowned into Libby's face. "Don't you like that idea?"

She wriggled. "I know it's ridiculous, but I feel a bit like the junior partner in this business. You're paying your way already."

"You didn't let me finish." Max stopped walking. "It's not just my skills the police are interested in, but yours as well. That business at the cathedral—"

"Didn't earn any money from that, did I?"

"But once again, you were ahead of the police. They've reorganised since Chief Inspector Arnold moved on. Joe's been promoted to detective inspector, and he's working for a new guy, Detective Chief Inspector Morrison."

"And I suppose this Morrison is one of your secret handshake Masonic Brotherhood."

Max laughed. "You know I'm not a Mason. Wasn't it Groucho Marx who said he'd never join a society that would have him as a member? I think that applies to me. Anyway, those days are pretty much over. The Chief Constable can't go further than saying they're interested in working with us, but they'd like to," he put on a pompous, official voice, "interview us with a view to retaining us both as consultants."

Libby felt a grin steal across her face. "Imagine that. It would make me feel like a proper investigator." She thought aloud. "Mandy's been doing well with the chocolate business, so I could pass more of that to her. Still, it doesn't help our decision. Are we going to investigate the mystery of why Liam Weston stole the ring?"

"Look on it as a chance to hone your skills," Max said. "You know you want to."

A little knot of excitement formed in Libby's stomach at the thought of working officially with the police. Maybe this private investigator business would work after all.

She jumped as Shipley tugged the lead. The dog's nose was close to the ground, following an interesting scent. Libby slid her hand through his collar. "Come on Shipley. You can't follow every rabbit down its hole." The dog ignored her.

She hauled on the lead, but the dog resisted, paws planted firmly on the grass. Max looked back. "What's bothering Shipley?"

"I don't know. Springers are bred as gun dogs.

When they catch a scent, they stop and point with their noses. I don't think Shipley's been trained for that, but he's inherited a great sense of smell. He can find things even Bear doesn't notice."

"Maybe we should let Shipley lead us. He seems very sure there's something interesting ahead. Maybe there are deer nearby."

Libby let the lead go slack. "Go on, old fellow. Show us what's bothering you."

Shipley, no longer constricted, crept forward with legs bent, his belly close to the grass. He led the way down through the trees towards the river, following a muddy path. As they rounded a bend, a small stone bridge appeared in the distance, spanning the water.

"What's that?" A splash of red, ruby bright, caught Libby's attention.

"Not sure." Max broke into a run. "Looks like an accident."

A tractor lay on its side where the bridge met the bank. Libby gasped. "There's someone underneath." Panting, she knelt by the man's side. "He's not dead, is he?"

"I'm very much afraid so." Max's fingers searched for a pulse.

Libby's stomach heaved. "Max, don't you see who it is?"

Max's face was grim. "I'm afraid I do. It's that

lad from the fight."

"Liam Weston. The farmhand who works for Mike. The one who stole the ring."

Max had his phone pressed to his ear, speaking to the police. Libby took a step back. The first time she'd found a body in Exham, she'd moved it. She still blushed at the memory. Joe Ramshore had been furious.

Still, it wouldn't hurt to look, as long as she didn't touch. Keeping her distance, she let her eyes run over every inch of Liam's body, from the baseball cap a few inches from his head, to a single battered brown boot. His other leg was twisted under his body.

Blood had trickled from a head wound and soaked into the ground, leaving ominous brown stains on the grass. Liam's eyes, sightless, stared up at the sky, where the lark still sang. Libby shivered.

Dividing the ground into imaginary quadrants, she tried to examine every tuft of grass with her eyes. Here and there, daisies poked cheerful heads above the grass. The ground was dry around Liam's body, since there had been no rain for days. She could see no sign of footprints.

Max called, "They're on the way."

Libby didn't reply. Something was glinting in the sunlight. She squinted. It was metallic and shiny. "Max, can you see?" She pointed.

"What is it?"

"I can't tell exactly, but it looks like a key. A tiny, gold key."

A car pulled up a hundred yards away, decanting the first police arrivals. Libby's fingers itched to pick up the key, but the police sergeant waved her away. In minutes, the area was sealed off with bright yellow tape, officers in white suits bent over the body and tractor. Photographers recorded every inch of the scene.

Libby's head swirled with questions.

***

"I'm afraid this has put the cart before the horse." An air of gloom suffused Detective Chief Inspector Morrison's long face. Sitting opposite Libby and Max at a plain wooden table in the police station, he sucked coffee through a voluminous moustache.

Libby's heart had returned to normal but she couldn't shift the sick feeling inside her stomach. She would never get used to seeing a dead body.

DCI Morrison took a Hobnob from the plate, sighed, bit into it and continued. "We were planning to meet with you to work out the kind of consultancy contract we need, according to all these EU rules and regulations we have to abide by for now." He sighed again. "It seems events have overtaken us, and you two have got yourselves involved already, so let's work together, see how things go, and use this nasty business as a trial run." He took another bite of the biscuit, sat back in his chair, and narrowed his eyes, watching Libby's reaction. She hoped her expression conveyed the right amount of interest and gave no sign of her internal wobbles.

Morrison pursed his lips, nodded once, sharply, and continued, "I'm the Senior Investigating Officer. Joe Ramshore will be leading the inquiry team, so you need to liaise with him. Max, I'm well aware he's your son, which is tricky, but I'll make sure that information goes up the line to the Commissioner, so there's no suspicion of nepotism."

Max nodded. "The last thing I want to do is tread on Joe's toes. I'm aware he's newly promoted and he'll want to do things properly."

Morrison rotated the biscuit in his hand, regarding it intensely, as though wondering whether it was poisoned. Libby debated whether the man was naturally melancholy, or whether his job had driven him to despair. "Of course. The police will handle all aspects of the investigation. Your role will be providing background checks where necessary. Be aware that at present this is an investigation into an accident."

Libby said, "Is there any evidence that it might be more than just an accident?"

The DCI took a long drink, replaced the mug on the table, and grimaced. "Our minds are open at the moment. Given your past record of finding murder victims even when all the evidence points towards an accident, we're not ruling anything out." His eyes were sharp. "I appreciate the low profile you've kept in the past, and the fact that your name rarely appears in the newspapers. I would very much like that to continue." The police officer was giving her a warning.

She smiled, as innocently as possible. "What are you expecting us to do?"

"Make use of your local knowledge. Find out whether there's any possibility of foul play. There are one or two points I've asked my team to follow up, even before the pathologist's report arrives. For example, there are several bruises on the body, especially the arms. The bruises match, as though someone grabbed hold of the victim from behind. They could have been made by a thumb and fingers."

Libby swallowed. "I suppose you know about yesterday's fight?"

Morrison's faint smile showed he already had that piece of information. Less than two hours since they'd found the body and Morrison was already well on top of things. "Why don't you fill me in?" he invited.

He was testing Libby's reliability. Joe must have told Morrison about the fight at the wedding. She'd better make sure she remembered accurately, or she'd find herself under suspicion. "It was a family thing," she began. "The bride's brother had an argument with Liam Weston about…" She hesitated, then ploughed on. "About a missing ring. It looks as though Liam had taken it from a rich aunt."

DCI Morrison nodded. "It could be nothing. Fights happen all the time at weddings. Young people pour beer into their stomachs and find any excuse to pick a quarrel. Too much testosterone, some of these lads."

There was a knock at the door. "Come in."

Joe appeared. "You sent for me, sir?"

Morrison unfolded his body from the chair. "I'll leave you to talk. Today's other priority, I'm afraid, is my input to the report on traffic violations. More than my job's worth to be late submitting that piece of vital information to my colleagues. Detective Inspector, you're in charge of managing this part of the investigation. He looked at Max and Libby through sad brown eyes.

"Remember what I said. If family business gets in the way it will be the end of our alliance."

CHAPTER FOUR

Dinner

"Supper tonight at my place." Max dropped Libby at her cottage. "We invited people round, remember? I'll pick you up about six?"

Libby groaned. "I'd forgotten. What was I thinking, planning a supper a couple of days after the wedding? I haven't cooked and there's nothing in the freezer…" Her memory kicked in. "Oh no. We've invited everyone; my friend Angela, Mandy and Reginald. And Claire's coming with Joe. I mean…"

Max laughed. "Don't look so guilty. I know what you mean. You're a little scared of Joe's wife, aren't you?" Claire was a psychiatric social worker; the kind of organised, professional woman that remembered appointments and made Libby nervous.

"I like Claire. She's very kind and terribly clever, but every time I meet her, I do something embarrassing, like throw up. And you can stop laughing, Max Ramshore.

"That wasn't your fault. You'd been poisoned, that day on the Levels. I'm sure Claire thinks you're wonderful."

She doubted that. "I'd like to show her I can do something properly, but it looks as though we'll be serving beans on toast tonight."

"Relax," Max advised. "We don't meet up to test your cooking. I'll order a take-away: onion dopiaza all round."

***

The friends had meant to spend the evening comparing photos of the wedding, but Liam Weston's death drove those plans out of everyone's heads and they talked of little else. Claire, tucking a strand of shiny hair behind an ear, held up a warning hand. "Don't forget, I'm no super sleuth, like the rest of you."

Mandy swallowed a mouthful of rice. "Not me. I mean to keep well away from the Ramshore and Forest private investigations."

Max scoffed, "You're Libby's right-hand man, young lady, and don't forget it." He paused. "Maybe I should say right-hand woman. Sounds odd, though."

Libby hardly registered the words. She'd stopped eating, a heaped fork waving, ignored, halfway to her mouth. Was it her imagination, or did Mandy seem unusually subdued? She stole a glance at Reginald, Max's American colleague. He'd appeared on the scene a few months ago, investigating thefts of ancient books, and Mandy had fallen for his southern charm. Libby wasn't surprised. The man was well over six feet tall, with a shaven head, enormous, sensitive hands and a dark brown voice to die for. She was almost sure his work in England, investigating the theft of valuable books on behalf of the International League of Antiquarian Booksellers, was coming to an end. Perhaps Mandy was already pining.

Max whisked away used plates and topped up the wine glasses. "What do people think? Are we looking at a murder?"

Libby said, "I know jumping to conclusions is one of my faults, but this time, I'm not so sure. Liam's death could easily be an accident. Tractors turn over far too often on farms."

Joe agreed. "All the signs are that Liam was careless. The ground slopes sharply by the river. If he was driving too fast, or misjudged just a little, the tractor wheels could have hit the edge of the bridge hard enough to topple it over."

"On the other hand," Max put in, "Liam was an experienced driver. He's worked on the farm for years. Why would he suddenly make a rookie mistake?"

Libby ran a finger round the top of her wine glass. "It was the day after that fight at the wedding. No one likes being accused of theft, and it would surely have preyed on Liam's mind. He'd probably had too much to drink at the reception, so he'd be suffering from a hangover as well as a few bruises from the fight, and he'd be worried Lady Antonia, or Tim, might go to the police about the ring."

Max turned to Joe. "Does he have a record of any sort?"

"A caution once, for being drunk and disorderly in Taunton after a night out. Apart from that, he's clean as a whistle."

"What about forensics?"

"Nothing yet. Without signs of foul play, the post-mortem isn't high priority, so we'll have to wait a day or two for results. I've asked for an analysis of the stomach contents and blood samples to see if he'd taken anything."

Libby asked, "What sort of thing?"

"A few of the young farmers around here take drugs," Joe pointed out. "There's a lot of depression in the industry. It's not just low milk prices, though that hasn't helped, but some of the farmers never got back on their feet after foot and mouth wiped out their herds."

Angela joined the discussion. She'd sat quietly until now, but she'd been born in Somerset and had an encyclopaedic knowledge of everyone in the county. "Liam didn't have business worries. He'd been working at Handiwater Farm while he saved up enough to start his own herd. Any worries about making a living would sit with Belinda and Mike."

Max smiled. "I think that gives us a clue where we need to start looking."

Libby was keen to visit Belinda after the woman's odd behaviour at the wedding. "I'll take a trip out to the farm and see how things are." She said nothing about Belinda's money worries. She'd told Max in confidence, as her business partner, but had no right to spread the information further. Belinda's talk of financial pressures had roused her curiosity and she'd like to know more about the farm. If it was in serious trouble, the farm workers would be worried about their jobs. Perhaps Liam, nervous about the future, had seen the ring in the grass and seized an opportunity to make some easy cash.

Joe sounded enthusiastic. "Maybe Max could do a little digging into the farm's financial affairs. I can't get a warrant for surrendering them to the police, but there'll be records available. After all, they're a limited company. They have to post accounts at Somerset House every year."

Claire, his wife, sat quietly as the others talked. She looked from one face to another, alert, following the conversation, but her eyes kept returning to Mandy. Libby hid a smile. Mandy wore two eyebrow rings, a stud in the middle of her lower lip, a cross attached to the side of her nose, and earrings that jangled loudly with every movement of the head. No wonder Claire found it hard to tear her eyes away.

The small frown creasing Claire's forehead deepened. Her gaze tracked to Mandy and back to Libby. Was she sending a message? Libby took a closer look at Mandy's face. A light film of sweat showed through the white powder on her nose and forehead. Libby spoke quietly. "Are you feeling unwell?"

Mandy stared at the table. "I'm fine." Her voice shook, and Claire raised an eyebrow. Libby gave a tiny nod, and as the others tucked into ice cream, they both watched Mandy. The young woman played with her food in silence, mixing sauce into rice and pushing it around the plate. Hardly a single spoonful reached her mouth.

Finally, even Reginald noticed her behaviour. "Mandy, I'm starting to worry whether it's safe to eat the food. You haven't swallowed anything. I guess you didn't doctor it in some way, when you were out in the kitchen?"

Mandy dropped her fork, shoved her chair back and staggered to her feet, rocking the table. Cutlery rattled and a drop of wine slopped over the rim of Libby's glass. Mandy's cheeks flamed as she gasped, "I didn't—I can't—" With a sob, she dashed the back of one hand across her eyes and ran from the room.

In the moment of shocked silence, Libby rose to follow, but Claire touched her arm. "Probably best to let her have a moment alone."

Concern was written all over Reginald's big, kind face. "I didn't mean to upset her."

"Have you told her you're going back to the States soon?" Libby asked. "You know she has a crush on you."

"Sure, she knows. We had a little thing going for a while, but it kind of fizzled. Mandy's spent the past few weeks telling me about that ex-boyfriend of hers. What's his name? Steve? I guess I've been something of a father figure. Just as well. I can't stand that music she listens to."

A knot of worry in Libby's stomach tightened as she remembered a conversation with Mandy, about a quarrel with Steve. "I was on the train to London," Mandy said. "Everything was fine. We were planning to eat at Steve's flat before going to a gig. I'd only got to Bristol, when a bunch of kids came on board the train. They were a bit noisy, like all kids, but they didn't even notice me." She'd made a strangled noise, like a failed laugh. "Suddenly, I couldn't breathe. Honest, Mrs F. I thought I was going to suffocate. We were just arriving in Bath and I was scared I'd faint in front of all those kids, so I kind of stumbled off the train and got a taxi home. Cost a fortune."

"Did you explain to Steve?"

Mandy had sniffed and shook her head. "I sent him a text, saying I couldn't make it. He was mad with me and we broke up." She never told Steve she'd been diagnosed with claustrophobia, and despite Libby's pleading, she'd refused to get help, and forbade any further discussion of the matter.

Judging by this evening's scene, it seemed Mandy's problems had not, as Libby had hoped, disappeared. Libby whispered, "Claire, could I have a word?"

She led the way into Max's study. Once there, second thoughts struck her dumb. Claire prompted, "You know something about Mandy, don't you? Can you give me a hint?"

Libby bit her lip. "I don't want to break a confidence."

"It's OK, Mrs F." Mandy had followed them into the room. "You're a psychiatric nurse, Claire, aren't you?"

Claire nodded. "Kind of. Do you want to talk?"

Mandy blew her nose.

Claire beckoned Mandy to an armchair. "Maybe, you'd better start at the beginning. The others can manage without us for a while."

Libby left them alone. Curiosity ate into her, but she had no business interfering. Neither spoke of their private conversation when they returned to the table. The other guests, with admirable discretion, managed to avoid any reference to Mandy's odd behaviour, instead making a great show of wondering about the tiny key found near Liam's body. Reginald spoke for them all when he said, "What in the world would a big guy like Liam Weston want with a tiny key like that?"

CHAPTER FIVE

Farm visit

Libby rose early next morning, planning to visit the farm. At least the trip would take Libby's mind off Mandy's woes, and maybe answer a few questions about Liam. She planned to take Bear and Shipley for the ride, hoping to borrow Max's Land Rover, for the dogs really wouldn't fit comfortably into her purple Citroen. Bear had often ridden in the back, overflowing the seat and drooling over Libby's headrest, but the notion of shoe-horning Shipley into the little car seemed a step too far.

Max, already seated at his computer, huge coffee cup alongside a substantial slice of Libby's ginger cake, glanced up through steel-rimmed glasses. "I'm checking the farm's public accounts." He took a giant bite of cake, gave a vague nod in answer to Libby's suggestion she take the car, waved an arm in her direction, and returned to his screen.

The road to the farm trailed for more than half

a mile through a patch of woodland, winding round fields of sheep, finally ending in a pristine farmyard. Libby wore wellies, expecting to wade through mud, but the stones of the yard were swept clean as a suburban patio. To one side a row of three quad bikes gleamed, chrome polished to a sparkle, paint spotless.

The farmhouse, long and low, was built of local Ham stone. The woodwork sparkled with fresh paint and crystal-clear windows reflected the bright summer sun. There was no sign the place suffered from lack of funds, as Belinda had suggested.

The dogs firmly secured on their leads, Libby rapped on the farmhouse door. No reply. She knocked once more, stepped back and gazed around for inspiration. The house was fronted by a small area devoted to vegetables and flowers and a tiny patch of lawn, but beyond, a metal gate led to a set of outbuildings. Libby tied the dogs to the gate and approached the nearest outbuilding.

She slipped through the door, hearing the gentle hum and rhythmic pumping of a milking parlour, smelling the warm scent of cattle. The black and white cattle took no notice of her arrival. They munched hay, apparently untroubled by the pumps attached to their udders. As the milking machinery purred to a halt, the gate at one end of the building clanged open to release the cows, lowing quietly, into a field. The gate closed behind the last animal and its partner at the other end opened to let more enter. Mike appeared at Libby's side. "Impressive, isn't it? It's our new robotic system. Hardly any need for me to be here. Not like the old days when we milked by hand."

Libby shook her head. "It's all so efficient."

The man grunted. "You thought I'd be sitting on a three-legged stool, my head against the cow's stomach, pulling on the teats by hand?"

Libby laughed. "I'm ashamed to say you're right. I'm a townie, at heart."

"Well, I don't suppose you came to watch our latest technology, did you?" Mike narrowed his eyes and wiped his hands on a hank of cloth.

"Take over, Jake, will you?"

An older man in brown overalls grunted as he passed from one cow to another, washing the udders. Mike leaned on the gate, gazing across his fields. "You found young Liam's body, I hear." He pulled off his cap, twisting it between calloused fingers. "A bad business, that. He'd been down that field many a time, and there are plenty of steeper slopes. Can't imagine what the lad was thinking, letting the tractor tip over. Must have been going too fast, I suppose, the young fool."

"I came to see Belinda, really. You know, see

if she's OK, what with that fight at the wedding, and then Liam's death. I thought she might be upset."

Mike Carmichael led Libby into the house, scratching the back of his head. "Ah, well now, you've missed Belinda. Gone to town, she has. Shopping therapy, she calls it. Can't think of anything worse, myself, but she reckons it's relaxing. Buying shoes, I reckon. Got a cupboard full, upstairs."

Mike gestured towards the kettle. "Tea?" Libby smiled, hiding a sense of unease. It seemed an odd time to go shopping, so soon after Liam Weston's accident. Belinda must be worried sick. Apart from distress at the sudden death of a young man she knew well, there were implications for the farm. The tractor might turn out to be faulty, or badly maintained. Health and safety inspectors would be involved, and the farm could end up in court.

Libby tried to be charitable. Perhaps Belinda needed to get away from her worries for a few hours. One thing was clear—she wouldn't be talking to Libby this morning.

"Bring the dogs in," Mike said. "We're used to muddy paws here."

Bear sprawled in front of the door while Shipley sniffed every corner of the kitchen, hoping for titbits. He was out of luck. The floor was immaculate and the room smelled of lemon-scented polish.

A square scrubbed table dominated the kitchen, an Aga and a deep Belfast sink were ranged along one wall, and an enormous, heavy-duty washing machine vibrated quietly nearby. Mike brewed tea, offering a mug of dark liquid and pushing a bowl of sugar across the table. Libby softened the tea with milk from a tall, white jug. "From your cows?"

Mike winked. "Raw milk, that is, straight from the cow. The best sort, but we're not allowed to sell it. No, every drop has to be pasteurised and sent off to the supermarkets, to sell for less than it costs to produce."

He peered at Libby under bushy eyebrows. Two vertical lines appeared on his forehead. "Now, maybe you've not come to see Belinda after all, Mrs Forest." His voice hardened. "Let's get down to brass tacks. You're here to find out about Liam, aren't you?"

Libby didn't bother to deny it. "I expect the police have visited?"

"Of course. They say there's no reason to suppose Liam's death is anything but an accident. Clumsiness, and too much to drink the day before, poor fellow. Ah. We'll miss the lad. He was a good worker." Mike's weather-beaten face, wrinkled and leathery from days in the sun, wind, and rain gave no clue to his real feelings.

Libby asked, "How long did Liam work here?"

"First came on the farm when he was a toddler. His ma used to bring him over to see Belinda. One of the Skinners, she was. Died a few years ago. Cancer or something. It was a bad time for young Liam. His dad went during the foot and mouth."

"Went? Left home, you mean?"

Mike's voice sounded bitter. "Not he. Did away with himself. Lost the farm, you see. The whole herd had to be slaughtered. Dumped in one great pit, set on fire, and buried over yonder." Mike waved an arm towards the window, where the rolling landscape stretched to the horizon. Libby shivered. One of those tranquil green pastures hid a grave full of the ashes of a man's livelihood and dreams.

"Liam, though, he still wanted to work on the land. He's been saving up, putting money aside, just about ready to start his own dairy herd, he told me. Not that there's profit to be had in milkers, not these days."

"I expect you have to diversify." Was that the right terminology?

Mike heaved a long sigh. "That's right. Can't

make a living from cattle, not these days. We rent out a couple of cottages down in the valley."

"It's a great place for tourists."

"That it is. Walking, that's the favourite. Too hilly in this part of Somerset for the cyclists, but camping and riding keep them coming. Then, there's Wimbleball Lake for water sports." For the first time, Mike grinned. "We make a good profit off the grockles, that's for sure. Come every year, some of them."

He lapsed back into silence. Libby prompted, "Then, there's cheese and yoghurt. I expect they're profitable?"

He shrugged. "We manage." His mouth clamped shut, making it clear any further discussion of his finances was off limits.

***

As Libby pondered her next question, a vehicle screeched to a halt in the yard. Mike stumbled to his feet without a word, opened the door, and left the kitchen, letting the door bang shut behind him. More surprised than offended, Libby stood by the window, out of sight of the two arrivals emerging from a mud-stained four-wheel drive.

One of the newcomers was female, a middle-aged woman in a Barbour jacket, faded hair straggling to her shoulders. It was the sight of her companion that sent a chill down Libby's back.

Xavier Papadopoulos, the grey man she'd met at the wedding reception, wore the loose trousers and kaftan of a would-be guru. A necklace of beads and feathers reached halfway down his chest as he towered above Mike, hovering like an eagle over a mouse. Mike seemed to shrink under the other man's gaze.

Libby leaned close to the window, listening, nerves jangling, butterflies circling her stomach. As the man's eyes slid over the house, she shrank back, hoping he hadn't noticed her peering from the window. Expressionless, he turned away towards the yard and Libby clicked her tongue, annoyed at her own edginess. She knew nothing about the man. He was tall, imposing, and oddly dressed, but that was no reason to fear the man. He'd done her no harm.

If only she could hear what they were saying. With a burst of determination, she shoved the door open. Why should she cower in the house as though she had something to hide? Squaring her shoulders, she stepped outside and smiled. "Hello. I'm Libby Forest." Her voice was too loud. She tried again, keeping her tone even. "We met at the wedding."

Mike turned and looked at her, his eyes so dark in a white face that Libby took an instinctive step back inside the house. Too late, she spotted Bear. Always ready to defend her, he'd crept close to her side and she stumbled against him, saving herself from a humiliating fall with a grab at the fur round his neck. Her right elbow hit the wall with a painful crack.

Regaining her balance, she lifted her chin, trying to retain some dignity. The grey man was openly smirking. Bear growled, the noise rumbling low in his chest, his lips quivering. He snarled, exposing sharp canines. "It's OK, Bear." Shipley stood still, alert, every muscle rigid.

Libby spoke to Mike. "The dogs are nervous."

The farmer blinked twice before replying, as though he found it hard to focus on Libby. "Did you hurt your elbow?" he asked at last.

Libby forced a smile, trying not to grimace. Her elbow burned, but she'd be dragged from the yard by wild horses before she'd admit it in front of Xavier Papadopoulos. "Not at all. I can see you're busy so I won't keep you. I'll come back when Belinda's here."

Xavier Papadopoulos stretched out his hand. The familiar voice was silky smooth. "Mrs Forest. It's a pleasure to meet again." He held Libby's hand a moment too long. Clenching her jaw, refusing to blink, she stared into intense grey eyes, until with a knowing smile the man dropped her hand.

It took an effort to overcome the instinct to wipe her palm on the seat of her jeans. Libby spoke to Mike. "Say hello to Belinda for me."

The farmer swallowed, looked at the floor, and muttered something indistinguishable about a quiz that Belinda wouldn't want to miss.

The visitor's companion had watched the brief pantomime without a word. Intrigued by her silence, Libby smiled. "I'm sorry, I didn't catch your name."

A nerve twitched in the woman's face. Before she could answer, Xavier Papadopoulos interrupted. "This is Olivia. My wife."

"Pleased to meet you." The atmosphere crackled with tension, and Bear slipped between Libby and the visitors.

Libby had rarely felt so unwelcome. "Thank you for the tea, Mike." She was reluctant to admit defeat. She'd be back. "Here's my card. Could you ask Belinda to phone me later? I'd like to talk to her about the wedding. We haven't had the chance for a good gossip."

Without reading the card, Mike slipped it straight into the pocket of his jacket. Libby felt three sets of eyes boring into her back as she loaded the dogs into the Land Rover, started the engine, and drove away.

She whistled, feeling pent-up strain seep from her body. "You dogs didn't care for Olivia and Xavier Papadopoulos any more than I did. The man gives me the creeps, and he dominates his wife. I wonder who they are and why Mike was suddenly so nervous when they arrived." She accelerated up the lane. "We need to do a little more sleuthing around the area. It's almost lunchtime. Let's find a local pub where dogs are welcome."

CHAPTER SIX

Local pub

At the end of Mike's long drive, signs pointed in two directions. One was labelled Compton Rival, the other Upper Compton. "Which do you think?"

Neither dog expressed a preference, so Libby turned left, towards Compton Rival. Less than a mile down the road, she passed the first of a small row of cottages. The terrace included half a dozen front doors and separate patches of ground, each defined by its owner's taste: one area packed with bean poles, raspberry canes, and strawberries; another covered with AstroTurf; and the third a riot of poppies, cornflowers, and hollyhocks.

An elderly man, hard at work in the vegetable garden, raised his head, leaned on a spade, and rubbed his back. Libby slowed the car and called, "Is there a pub in the village?"

The gardener chuckled and pointed a bony, earth-stained finger along the road. "You're almost there, m'dear, if you're looking for the Red Cow. Go on a bit further and you'll find the Gate Hangs

High. Take your pick."

Libby thanked him and let in the handbrake. How could two pubs in the same tiny hamlet make a living? As promised, she arrived at the Red Cow as she rounded the first corner. She drew up in front of the pub. Baskets crammed with cheerful lobelia, petunias, and fuchsias hung on the wall, and a vast tin bowl full of water sat beside the door. "This will do nicely," Libby told the dogs. "It seems you're welcome here."

She unlatched a heavy wooden door and pushed it open, breathing in the country-pub smell of real ale, years of wood fires, and floor polish. Cool and dark, in contrast to the vivid light of the midday sun outside, the room at first appeared deserted, but as Libby's eyes grew accustomed to the dim light she spotted a woman behind the bar. A little older than Libby, dressed in a tight, low cut, pink blouse with copious frills round the neckline, the woman polished the spotless bar with a bright yellow duster. "Come in, do. What can I get for you?"

At last, someone was pleased to see them. Libby could have hugged the bartender. "Are you serving lunch yet?"

"Anytime." The woman pointed to the wall. "The specials are on the board."

Libby deliberated, ordered a soft drink and a

goat's cheese and red onion tart, and chose a seat at a small round table. Situated in the bay window, she could watch the road. Any sign of the Papadopoulos couple and she'd be out of the place in a second.

The woman bustled round, adding knives and forks, glasses and napkins to each table. "You're not from round here, are you?" Her voice was cheerful. "On your holidays?"

Libby smothered a sigh. Holidays were a thing of the distant past. "I live in Exham," she confessed. "I'm just enjoying the countryside today. It's my day off." If only that were true. "Lovely out here, isn't it?"

The woman leaned on the bar, ready to chat. "Full of summer visitors, at the moment. This place will be heaving in half an hour. You've arrived just in time to beat the rush."

"I've been visiting Handiwater Farm. I expect Belinda and Mike come in here quite often?"

The woman shook her head. "Not them. They go to Upper Compton."

"The two villages are very separate, then?"

The woman gave a fruity chuckle and settled her blouse more comfortably on her shoulders. "I should say so. Them at Upper Compton think themselves a cut above those of us down here in Compton Rival. They wouldn't be seen dead in this old pub."

Libby looked around. "But it's lovely. They're missing a treat."

"Nice of you to say so." A bell pinged behind the bar. "That's your dinner ready."

Libby tucked into her tart, enjoying the raspberry dressing on the salad and making a mental note to make something similar at home. A group of three walkers arrived, equipped with boots and rucksacks, and sat at a nearby table. The barmaid organised their drinks and food, and Libby was left to wonder, in silence, why the two villages should so dislike each other.

Bear and Shipley had emptied the water bowl at the door and now sat at her feet, watching with unblinking eyes as the newly arrived humans tucked in to plates of steak, alert for any food that might fall on the floor. Libby finished her meal and returned to the bar. "Is there anything I can give the dogs? I've been out longer than I intended and they're hungry."

"Of course, my dear." She pattered behind the bar, returning with a dish of beef scraps. "There, that should do. Nice dogs." She sniffed. "They'll not be welcome in Upper Compton, you know. That Zavvy Papadopoulos and his wife will see to that."

Libby kept her tone light. "I met them earlier

today."

The barmaid puffed air between her lips in a show of disgust. "You don't want to have much to do with them. Think they own the county, they do, living in that old house. That Olivia comes from one of the oldest families round here, and Coombe House belongs to her. She was a pretty girl back in the day. You wouldn't know it from the look of her now, but they say you grow to look like your husband, don't they? Or is it your dogs?" She looked from Libby to Bear and chuckled. "Olivia used to get on all right with the rest of us, until she met that Zavvy and had her head turned."

"Unusual name for this part of the world, Papadopoulos."

The bartender polished knives with a bright yellow tea towel. "Olivia met him on a Greek island. Had a holiday in one of those retreats, where you go to lose weight, or stop smoking, or some such. I don't hold with that sort of nonsense, myself. People with too much money and not enough sense or willpower to sort out their own lives, if you ask me. I heard."

She leaned across the bar and dropped her voice to a whisper. "I heard Olivia had a problem." She glanced round the room, leaned closer, and hissed, "Drugs, you know."

She dipped glasses in a bowl of frothy water, dried them on her towel until they squeaked, and hung them in a wooden rack over the bar. "That's why her family sent her out there. They got more than they bargained for when she came back from Greece with Zavvy. Nasty piece of work, he is. Wouldn't be surprised if he was at the bottom of Liam Weston's accident."

"You've heard about that, then."

"All round the village. We don't keep no secrets out here. Poor young fellow, Liam. Nothing but bad luck in that family."

"His parents' farm went bust in the foot and mouth, or so I heard…"

The barmaid took a long look at Libby. The friendly smile had evaporated. She sucked her teeth. "You heard that, did you? Got a good grapevine?" She turned away to polish the Exmoor Ale beer pump with a vigour that signalled the end of the conversation. Libby called the dogs and made her way to the door. She'd asked one question too many. The barmaid showed every sign of regretting her earlier gossip.

As Libby reached the door, the woman coughed, glanced round at the walkers and muttered. "Liam's dad's farm was a mile down the road in that direction." She flicked her head to the right. "Just the farmhouse left now, on the edge of

Upper Compton. If you go down there, you watch your step. Make sure those dogs are with you. You can't be too careful."

Libby drove back the way she'd come, passing the lane leading to Mike's farm. Half a mile later she came to a tumbledown brick building set back from the road, on the edge of the next village. Curious, she stopped the car and walked across, peering through cracked windows into desolate, neglected rooms.

There was nothing else to see, and certainly no evidence to suggest she needed the dogs' protection. What had the barmaid meant by her warning? Was she talking about Liam's dilapidated old family home, or was there danger in Upper Compton, where the unpleasant Papadopoulos couple ruled the roost?

CHAPTER SEVEN

Mandy

Still unsettled by the unpleasant episode with Mike and his visitors, Libby was glad to spend the next morning in the Exham bakery with Mandy. Frank, the baker, had rearranged their schedule so Libby and Mandy spent one day a week working together. Delighted with the recent improvement in the fortunes of the bakery, mostly as a result of the popularity of Libby's cake recipes and luxury chocolates, Frank was keen to encourage Mandy in her training.

This afternoon, the supervisor from the local further education college was planning a visit. In a couple of weeks, Mandy would be taking her first exam, on the route to a qualification in catering. Libby offered to rearrange the meeting, to give Mandy a chance to recover from her breakdown at supper, but her apprentice turned down the offer. "I'm fine, Mrs F. I don't know what came over me."

"Don't worry. If you need anything from me,

just ask. Otherwise we'll carry on as normal."
Mandy hadn't confided in Libby about her talk
with Claire, and Libby knew her apprentice better
than to ask too many questions.

Mandy moved around the kitchen, as though
unable to keep still. "To tell you the truth, Mrs F,
I'm nervous about this afternoon."

"Well there's no need to worry. You're doing a
great job in the business. I'm sure you'll sail
through the supervisor's questions with no
difficulty."

Mandy's laugh sounded shaky. "I'd rather be
selling chocs to shops than answering questions. I
was hopeless at school. Not a single qualification."

"Well, this is your chance to shine, because I'll
be writing a great report on your progress. You've
been a real asset."

Mandy's cheeks turned pink. "Thanks, Mrs F."
She took a very deep breath. Libby kept busy,
stacking chocolate boxes on shelves, saying
nothing, sensing Mandy had something to say.
"That Claire," Mandy ventured, "she says I could
talk to one of her therapist friends about this
claustrophobia problem of mine." She
pronounced the word with care. "Claire says it's
more common than people imagine. She reckons
it's easy to deal with, in just a few sessions."

Libby nodded, wishing Mandy had taken her

advice months ago and asked for professional help. She'd been more distressed by Mandy's panic attack the other evening than she'd admitted. Now, it looked as though it was a blessing in disguise. "I think that's a great idea. Claire knows what she's talking about."

"She says I don't need to worry about seeing a psychiatrist every week for a year, like I thought. She says I'm not mad. I just got into bad habits."

"Sounds very positive. Have you got an appointment?"

"That's the trouble. I'm going to have to pay for the sessions or go to my GP and wait months for an appointment." Mandy glared at Libby. "And don't you even think of offering to pay. You've done more than enough for me already and I can just about afford the first few sessions."

Recognising the challenge in Mandy's over-bright eyes, Libby bit her tongue. "Who's the therapist? Anyone in Exham?"

"Someone called Julia Enders." The bakery bell clanged as the door swung open. Mandy hissed, "Lives in Bath. I'll go after my next visit to Jumbles. They want to see some more chocolate samples this week."

The new arrival in the shop, an unfamiliar young man, interrupted. "Julia Enders, did you say? Why, I know her very well."

Libby stitched a cool smile on her face. "Can I get you something?" she asked.

The man ignored her, focusing on Mandy. "Well, you're a sight for sore eyes. Haven't seen a proper Goth for ages. Didn't know they still existed in this backwater."

Libby, offended by the sneer in his voice, shot a glance at Mandy, praying the young woman would hold on to her temper. Mandy, though, wore a broad smile. "Hello, Peter. Long time no see."

Libby said, "You two know each other? Don't tell me, you were at school together." There was only one secondary school in Exham, and every long-time resident knew all the others and their families. When Libby first arrived in town, she'd been like a stranded goldfish in the close community. Many still regarded her as an outsider.

Mandy giggled. "This is Peter."

"And you must be the famous Mrs Forest." The young man's feet were set wide apart, his hands in his pockets; he seemed altogether too self-assured for Libby's taste.

Mandy, though, had brightened up at his appearance. "How do you know Julia Enders?"

"Friend of my uncle." He winked. "A very good friend, if you know what I mean. What do you know about her?"

Mandy hesitated. "I suppose there's no reason to keep it a secret. I'm going to see her about my phobia." The defiant gleam in her eyes sent a warm glow of almost maternal pride through Libby.

Peter looked Mandy up and down. "You're the last person I'd expect to have a phobia. You beat me up in the school playground, just because I called you a stupid Goth, remember? What's this phobia then? Spiders?"

Libby hated the sarcasm in his voice, but Mandy laughed. "Claustrophobia actually. Can't travel in trains and coaches. Nothing mega."

"Well, Julia deals with all kinds of phobias. She reckons to shift 'em in one session."

He lounged against the counter, munching a doughnut. "Julia says she can re-programme your brain to help you overcome learned anxieties, or some such palaver. Works for all sorts of mental problems, apparently—" He broke off, wiping sugar from his chin, as the door swung open again with a jaunty jangle, and the owner of the flower shop appeared.

Libby stifled a sigh. The woman was one of the worst gossips in town, and from the look on her face she'd caught the end of Peter's sentence. A busy shop was really the worst place to talk about serious subjects. "Phobias? If you're talking about alternative remedies," the florist began, "I can tell you what to do. My sister had a dreadful fear of lifts, because she was shut in a cupboard by mistake when she was a child. The hinges were on the inside, and she couldn't get out for an hour. Her mother broke the door down with a hammer in the end..." Mandy's mouth hung open. Her eyes opened wide as the woman went on, "My sister went to a fortune teller at the County Show and the woman picked up on the problem. She saw my sister a few times..."

Mandy sounded breathless. "What did she say?"

The florist shook her head. "Can't remember what it was exactly. Something to do with eggs. Or was it candles? Anyway, she was cured in a shake of a rat's tail."

Libby began, "I really don't think we need a fortune teller," but Mandy's eyes gleamed. "I've always wanted to have my fortune told. Who was it at the fair? Was it a local person?"

"She lives over Dunster way, I think," the flower shop lady replied. "I can let you have her address, if you like. She's not usually a fortune teller, of course. That's just for the shows. She's what they call an alternative therapist."

"Mandy, I really think you should stick to this Julia, if Claire recommended her. You know she's properly trained, and…"

Mandy was too busy making a note of the alternative therapist's address to listen. Libby's heart sank. Her young friend was grabbing any idea that came her way. Maybe it was best to end the conversation here, before another customer arrived with an even more ridiculous suggestion. She served the flower shop lady. "Your usual sandwich?"

Peter, Mandy's old school friend, watched with a superior half-smile playing on his lips. Libby's hand itched to slap the smug face. Instead, she said, "I take it you've just arrived back in Exham, if Mandy hasn't seen you before today."

Peter grinned. "I'm sizing up the opposition."

"I'm sorry? What opposition?"

"I work for Terence Marchant. We're opening a new patisserie in Exham and Terry asked me to look at the local cafes and sandwich shops. Of course, our place will be rather different. More focused on croissants and macaroons than cheese and pickle sandwiches. I don't think you've got anything to fear."

Mandy's face turned pink. "You mean, you're a spy? Then you can get out of here, Peter Morris. I never liked you when we were at school and I was right. And I won't be visiting any therapist you know."

Peter smirked harder. "No need to get in a tizz. We don't want to make your phobias worse, do we?"

Libby's heart hammered. Her instincts had been right. She'd known the lad was bad news as soon as he came in. His trousers were shiny and much too tight, and his hair slick with grease. She held the door open. "Thank you for coming in, Mr Morris. You can tell your boss we're managing very well, and there's plenty of room for all kinds of shops in Exham."

Peter used his elbow to shove himself off the counter, swallowed the last of his doughnut, and snorted. "You can go on selling your buns, Mrs Forest, and your home-made chocolates. Terry thinks there might be a place for them in the patisserie. Of course, they'll need to be of professional quality. I expect he'll pop in one of these days for a sample, and you'd do well to offer your best products. He's quite the businessman. You'd best stay on the right side of him."

As the door closed, Libby let out an angry whistle. "So, Terence Marchant thinks he might possibly be interested in my chocolates." Her voice was heavy with sarcasm. "How very kind of him. I think we'd better tell Frank what's going on. Between you and me, and despite what I said, I think Exham has just about as many food outlets as it can manage. Do you think we should be worried?"

Mandy gave a short, unconvincing laugh. "I'm sure this place is popular enough to beat off Peter Morris and his boss. Is Terence Marchant anything to do with the cat lady in Wells?"

"He's the rich son. I was worried about her, and I visited him to discuss all those cats she keeps. He told me he might start a rival business in Exham. I thought he was just winding me up, but it seems I was wrong."

More customers arrived. As Libby served, she watched Mandy from the corner of her eye. The young woman kept staring at the address and phone number of the alternative therapist. If only there was something Libby could do. An unqualified therapist could lead to trouble, but she knew better than to try to stop Mandy. Opposition would only make her more determined. Libby added it to the mental list of things to worry about in the middle of the night when she couldn't sleep. The list seemed to be growing fast. "Can you manage here for an hour or so, Mandy? I'd like to call round to see Frank. I know it's his day off, but he needs to know about Terence Marchant's patisserie as soon as possible."

***

Libby was disappointed to find Frank away from home. She rang his mobile number, but he didn't answer. It was no surprise. He'd never come to terms with mobile technology. Libby shrugged. He'd taken a few days off. He rarely spent more than twenty-four hours away from his beloved bakery, but it was fully staffed for the next few days and he'd be back soon enough. Terence Marchant's new shop wouldn't be opening for a week or two.

Libby slipped a note through the door, asking Frank to get in touch when he returned home, and spent the rest of the day with Mandy in the bakery. The college catering supervisor arrived, questioning Mandy about food hygiene and health and safety. Pleased with the apprentice's progress, she left clutching a bag of Belgian buns left over from the lunchtime rush.

Mandy beamed. "She says I'm doing really well." She'd removed the rings from her face and ears in honour of the supervisor's visit, and apart from purple lipstick could pass for any attractive young woman, so long as she stayed behind the counter. The Doc Martens on her feet gave the game away, though. Libby wondered if the supervisor had noticed them.

At the end of the day, when the shop was

clean and shiny, Libby and Mandy took off their overalls and prepared to shut the shop. "My feet are killing me," Libby muttered. "It's these stupid kitten heels. Maybe I should get some boots, like yours."

"You could do worse, Mrs F. Lots of space for the toes."

As Mandy dug into the pocket of her overall and dropped the little pile of pencil, paper, and handkerchief on the counter, Libby peeked at the address of the alternative therapist.

Abbott House, near Upper Compton, she read, and a shiver crept down her spine. That was the village the barmaid had mentioned, where Mike's creepy visitors, Olivia and Xavier Papadopoulos, lived. Libby didn't want them anywhere near Mandy. Despite her determination to stay out of her apprentice's private life, she had to say something. "That address…"

Mandy raised an eyebrow. "Yes?" Her tone was belligerent.

Libby opened and closed her mouth several times. The urge to stop Mandy was almost overwhelming, but she knew it would be a mistake. Already, Mandy's eyes glowed with the light of battle. "Are you planning to visit?"

Mandy shrugged. "Yes, but I don't know how I'm going to get there."

The cold hand of fear grabbed hold of Libby's insides. She didn't want Mandy getting involved with this therapist and she hated the thought of her visiting Upper Compton on her own.

She thought quickly. "You know, we haven't taken delivery of that new vehicle I ordered. Remember, I said I'd get another car for the business. You did well to pass your driving test first time, and you can drive it when it arrives, but in the meantime if you really want to go over to see this woman, I'd like to come with you. We can go in the Citroen and take Bear. I always feel better in a strange place when he's around."

Mandy's face was difficult to read, but she was fond of the dog, so Libby ploughed on. "I think we should leave Shipley behind. He's still a bit wild. In fact, the vet's running some advanced classes for crazy dogs, and I'm planning to take him, soon. Meanwhile, if you really insist on visiting this woman in Upper Compton, I'll take you." That way, she could keep an eye on her apprentice. Keep her out of harm's way. They'd both be fine, with Bear in tow.

Mandy picked up her phone. "Thanks, I'll ring and see if I can make an appointment for tomorrow. It's our half day."

CHAPTER EIGHT

Abbott House

Mandy's appointment with the alternative therapist was set for three the next afternoon. She spent the morning on the telephone at the bakery, cold calling likely distributors of Mrs Forest Chocolates. Libby was impressed. She hated trying to sell things to strangers. "They can always say no," Mandy pointed out. "Anyway, your chocs are so scrummy, I know they'll love them."

"Well, if you don't need me to help, I'll leave you to it. I've arranged a meeting with the vet to talk about Shipley."

"The obedience classes?"

"Exactly. Shipley's a beautiful dog, and he's won prizes for best in breed at the local show, but he wouldn't win anything for his behaviour."

As though to prove her right, Shipley darted round her feet, yapping and whining, wildly over-excited, when she collected him from Max's house. Once inside her little purple car, he sniffed every corner, snuffling for evidence of his best friend,

74

Bear.

Max held the car door as Libby calmed the dog, offering a chew. "That animal has an over-developed sense of smell," he said.

The vet was delighted to see Shipley, and the dog responded by leaping wildly around, despite Libby's stern commands. Tanya turned her back on the dog. "I won't encourage him," she said. "Now, you wanted to talk about obedience classes. Let's go inside. Come on, Shipley, walk to heel." To Libby's astonishment, the dog stopped leaping and barking and walked sedately, close to the vet's ankles.

"How did you do that?"

"He likes authority. The advanced training classes start tomorrow. I don't run them, I get an ex-police dog trainer to do that. He's like the dog whisperer and he'll soon sort Shipley out."

Libby said, "I rather suspect I need as much help as Shipley. Bear was well trained before I met him and the only other animal I've ever owned is Fuzzy. My cat. And she does exactly what she likes."

The vet laughed. "You mean your delightful marmalade. The one who broke her leg? How does she feel about Shipley?"

"When he's around, she hides in the airing cupboard. If he gets too near, she makes a swipe at his nose, but she only comes out to see Bear, these days. She worships that dog."

"Poor cat. The sooner Shipley falls into line, the better. Can you make the class tomorrow morning?"

"I wouldn't miss it for the world. Officially, Max owns Shipley as well as Bear, but I think he'll be delighted if I take the training off his hands." *And it will buy me a little more time to decide what I really want.*

***

Even Bear seemed subdued as Libby and Mandy arrived in Upper Compton. The village was bigger and less cosy than its smaller relative down the road. There was no welcoming pub, bright with summer flowers, just a featureless brick building close to the road, with no room for outside tables and chairs. Libby felt no temptation to eat there.

Her heart sank lower with every yard they covered, until the car crawled round the increasingly twisty lanes leading to Abbott House. Mandy's hands were clasped tight in her lap. She was as nervous as Libby.

"Are you sure about this?"

Libby wished her young friend would change

her mind, but Mandy shook her head. "I'm going to beat this phobia."

Libby fell silent, determined not to keep recommending Claire's therapist friend, but she felt heavy with trepidation. *This is a mistake.*

They followed the directions of the Satnav, enunciated in perfect Received Pronunciation by the invisible female. Libby imagined her as Charlotte, a wealthy woman lying on a chaise longue, sipping champagne between announcements.

As they drew nearer to Abbott House, even Charlotte sounded unsure, describing the road as an Unnamed Lane. The hedges grew closer until Libby's Citroen touched vegetation on both sides. Brambles scraped along the paintwork, setting Libby's teeth on edge, as the ground dipped sharply down into a valley.

"I hope we don't meet a horsebox." Mandy's voice trembled.

Just as Libby began to suspect the house they sought was some kind of joke perpetrated by the Exham flower shop woman, she saw a building. Tiny, half-hidden by over-hanging elm trees whose dense canopy of leaves shut out all but the most persistent rays of the sun, it was nothing like the grand mansion she'd expected. "I suppose this must be it?"

Mandy peered out of the window. "The name's on the gate."

Neither she nor Mandy was in a hurry to leave the familiar safety of the car, but Bear was restive, never content to sit quietly in a stationary vehicle. Libby climbed out and reluctantly led the way to the house.

The door flew open. "Ah, Mandy. There you are." Once more, Libby's expectations were confounded. She'd imagined a fairground fortune teller in tasselled shawls, gold bracelets, and a beaded head-dress. Kate Stephenson was a tiny, energetic woman in denim dungarees over a white t-shirt, with a blue square tied round her head. Fair curls escaped, framing delicate features. She wore no jewellery at all. "Sorry about the clothes." She laughed. "I've been trying to clean the house while the kids are at school." She bent over Bear, and he allowed her to stroke his head.

The tension-ache at the back of Libby's neck subsided. She shot a sideways glance at Mandy, who returned a sheepish grin. They'd both let imagination run away with them.

Instead of taking them inside, Kate Stephenson led the way round the corner of the house, under a wooden arch in the even deeper shade of a sturdy yew. The tree's wide trunk spoke of great age. There was something about yew trees. What was it, now?

As they reached the back of the house, Libby remembered. Yew trees were traditionally planted at the entrance to cemeteries. The wooden entrance was the lychgate. Sure enough, rows of discoloured gravestones marched down the garden. The quiet of the surrounding woods was broken by rooks, rising up, cawing and flapping. Under the noise, water babbled gently.

They followed a path between the graves, towards the corner of the garden where a summer house stood, doors flung wide, offering a glimpse of white-painted interior. "I hope you're not bothered by the old gravestones," Kate said. "Some of them date back to the seventeenth century. The cottage used to belong to the sexton who dug the graves. My boys and I love it here, living among the departed."

Libby gulped and followed her into the summer house. White walls reflected the daylight streaming through enormous windows. A small, round table stood in the centre of the room, with four comfortable-looking chairs pulled close. A pink sofa and a second, rectangular table against the far wall completed the furnishings.

"Have a seat." Kate smiled, showing a set of perfect, white teeth. "Don't worry, I'm not a witch, by the way. I only do fairground work for fun."

Her bright green eyes sparkled as though she sensed Libby's antagonism and found it amusing. Bear settled next to the pink sofa, his gaze following every one of Kate Stephenson's moves. Libby slipped a finger through his collar and sat close, glad he was there.

Kate turned her attention to Mandy. "Of course, you're the one needing my help. I can tell by your aura."

"My aura?" Mandy's brows met over her nose.

Kate laughed, the sound as musical as the murmur from the nearby stream. "Nothing scary. Everyone has their own aura, and it changes according to mood. Yours is a little orange today. You're anxious, of course." She bustled round the room, brewing something in a small pot with a bamboo handle. "Don't you love the way the Japanese make tea? I've been to Japan and seen the tea ceremony. They're completely mindful through the whole process."

Mandy nodded, eyes dark, face serious, but Libby stifled a groan. Max had once described mindfulness as a pseudo-scientific way of justifying the art of doing nothing. She'd argued at the time, but Kate's mention of auras and tea ceremonies within five minutes of their arrival left Libby cold. She subsided into the comfy cushions of the sofa and drank green tea.

Kate sipped from her cup in silence. Birds chattered outside. Somewhere, a clock ticked. Libby tried not to make slurping noises.

At last, Kate said, "Now, Mandy, let me help you."

Mandy peered around the room. "Don't you use a crystal ball, or tarot cards, or something?"

"No need. I can already sense your troubles, Mandy. You've had a difficult life. A broken home."

"Well, only recently. It was fine when I was a kid."

"Of course, it seemed fine to you. Both your parents were at home and you thought they were happy. Children always make the best of things. But, underneath, you knew something was wrong."

Kate paused. Mandy stammered, "W-well, I suppose I knew Mum was nervous around my dad. But I never saw him lay a hand on her. Not then. Not when I was small."

"She hid it from you, to protect you. Then, there was the thing you were scared of…"

Mandy's head jerked up.

"What was it, now? Something in the house…"

This time, the pause dragged on until Mandy broke into the quiet, her voice small and scared.

"The attic." She chewed on her lower lip. "There was a ladder that led up to the loft. Mum and Dad kept old curtains and bits of carpet there. I wasn't supposed to go up on my own."

"Your father stopped you, didn't he?"

"He told me I'd fall through the floorboards."

"But you wanted to see it?"

"That's right. So, one day, I went up there, and he caught me, and he was so mad." Kate laid her hands on Mandy's, tightly clasped on the table. "I expect you thought it was your fault."

"It was. You see, there were boxes up there. It was dark, up in the attic. It smelled musty, from the old curtains, I suppose, and there were boxes I'd never seen before. Some were just old clothes. You know, my baby clothes. Mum must have kept them. At the back of all the other boxes, I found a small one. It was different from the others–smaller, made out of painted wood."

Mandy's lip trembled as she continued, "I had this awful feeling before I opened it. I don't know what I expected to find, but I had to look. They were photos. Horrible pictures. Dad had been in the Bosnian war, you see, in 1995, just before I was born. The photos were terrible – picture of dead people. Some were soldiers, but others were just ordinary people. Women and children too. Covered in blood, a-and lying in heaps."

Libby closed her eyes. Mandy's father, Bert, was a bully. Once, when Mandy was lodging with Libby, he'd got drunk and tried to break into the house to find his daughter. Libby had no idea he'd once been a soldier. A bad time in Bosnia could explain his violent moods.

Kate said, "Did your father know you found his photos?"

Mandy nodded. "He caught me looking at them, and he was furious. He shouted, and then he started to cry." Her voice shook. Kate offered her a box of tissues. "Is that why I don't like small spaces? Because of the attic?"

Kate replaced the tissues on the table, near Mandy. "We can't be sure, at the moment, but it made a big impression on you. We need to talk more, another time, but if that experience started your fears, you'll begin to feel different, already."

Mandy was nodding. "I never thought about it like that, before." She screwed the tissue into a ball. "Do you think that might be why Dad… Why he…" Her voice faded away.

"You can say it, here. You're safe."

Mandy took a deep, shuddering breath. "That's why Dad used to hit Mum, isn't it? He was angry all the time and he took it out on her." She spoke slowly, as though thinking it through, her voice growing in confidence. "It wasn't my fault at all, was it?"

Kate smiled. "No. Not your fault."

Libby was astonished. She knew about Mandy's claustrophobia, and she'd seen her father's anger, but she'd never imagined there could be a link. She'd heard of soldiers suffering from mental health problems, even years after they left the army. Post-traumatic stress disorder. That's what it was called.

Kate sat back. "That's enough for now, Mandy. We'll talk some more, another time. There are bad things in your family's past, and we need to uncover them. It will take careful thought. I'll consider how best to handle it. You come back in a few days. I'm sure I can help you."

She led them through the cemetery-garden. "Perhaps you'll be able to come alone, next time?" she suggested. Libby narrowed her eyes, searching Kate's face, suddenly uneasy, but the warm smile was still in place and the woman's green eyes were wide. "You can bring a friend if you wish, but sometimes it's easier to talk when it's just the two of us."

She turned to Libby. "Give my regards to Max, when you see him. I knew him once, many years ago."

Libby started. Max had never mentioned Kate. Well, she couldn't expect to know everything about him. That was part of his charm, wasn't it?

Anyway, Kate was still talking. "I heard about Debbie. That she died. If you like, you can tell Max how sorry I am. I'll understand if you'd rather not."

***

As Libby and Mandy climbed back into the Citroen, Bear scrambling into the back seat, Libby broke the silence. "Are you OK?"

Mandy nodded, but still said nothing. The silence continued as Libby started the car, the engine juddering in protest. The steep slope and muddy ground were almost too much for the aging vehicle.

Mandy pulled out a tube of mints. "Want one?" Libby shook her head. Mandy sucked noisily. "Who's Debbie?"

Libby hesitated. Max had trusted her with the story of his daughter's death in a horse-riding accident. In a town like Exham, where everyone knew their neighbour's business, Libby was amazed no one had ever mentioned it to her. She supposed Max had worked hard to keep it private. Joe, as well, for Debbie had been his sister. Libby struggled for the right words. Although she often listened to gossip in her work, she tried not to fall into the trap herself.

The car lurched as a stray branch scraped along the driver's side, and Libby made up her mind. "I can't share it with you, Mandy. It's something that happened to Max many years ago. He would have to tell you himself."

"OK, no problem."

Libby shot a sideways glance at the set of her companion's jaw. Mandy didn't usually give in so easily. Probably, she was still thinking about today's session with Kate Stephenson. It had certainly left Libby confused. Set to distrust the so-called alternative therapist, she'd been astonished by the ease with which the woman uncovered some of Mandy's fears. Perhaps she'd been too hasty.

As Libby persuaded the car round a dog-leg bend, she came face to face with a heavy Range Rover. Both vehicles drew to a halt, the lane too narrow to allow them to pass.

Xavier Papadopoulos glared from behind the car's wheel. The nearest passing place was ten yards or so behind his vehicle. For a long moment, Libby's eyes locked with his in a silent battle. It was his responsibility to reverse and she wasn't going to let the man intimidate her into giving way. She'd have to travel backwards and negotiate the tricky bend. She waited, jaw set, stomach churning.

The stand-off seemed to last for hours. At last, the Range Rover scraped into reverse gear. With a glare that sent shivers down Libby's spine, Xavier Papadopoulos crunched his gears into reverse and shot backwards with wheels squealing. Swerving just far enough inside the passing place, he let Libby's Citroen squeeze through the gap. Bear barked, loudly, as Libby waved her thanks.

Mandy giggled. "Well, Mrs F. I wouldn't want to argue with you with that look on your face."

CHAPTER NINE

St Mary's

Next day, Max and Libby left the Land Rover under a tree in a pretty Exmoor village. "Why are we here?" Libby asked. "Upper Compton is still a few miles away." Max linked his arm with hers. "I want you to meet someone. First, though, tell me about your adventures with the alternative therapist."

They strolled down the lane, Bear and Shipley snuffling for rabbits in the hedgerow. Libby grunted. "I can't decide whether Kate Stephenson has some sort of psychic gift, or is playing tricks. The session with Mandy wasn't at all as I expected. I thought there'd be more jingling silver bracelets and patchouli oil, but instead, we sat very sedately and drank tea. It seemed to help Mandy, which I suppose is a good thing, but Kate made me nervous. She seemed to know everything."

Max gazed across the hedges towards empty green fields leading down into the valley. "Don't let your imagination run riot. She knew Mandy's name. It would be the easiest thing in the world for her to find out about Mandy's father. He's been in court. That would be reported in the papers and you'd be able to find reports on the internet. Given that knowledge, it wouldn't take too much work to uncover his background in the army and come up with a convincing story for Mandy."

"Maybe." Libby had learned to trust the knot of anxiety that formed in her stomach. It nearly always meant something was wrong. When she ignored that tiny ache, bad things often followed. "Kate, the therapist, or whatever she's called, said something odd, by the way. She sent you her best wishes." Libby kept her eyes steadily on the road ahead. "You didn't mention knowing her."

"I don't know her." Max sounded perfectly calm. They walked on a few paces. "What was her last name?"

"Stephenson."

He shrugged. "No, doesn't mean anything to me."

"But she knows you. She mentioned Debbie."

"What?" Max swung to face Libby, his eyes wide. Libby twirled a leaf in her fingers, trying to appear casual. Max rubbed a hand over his face. "Let me think. Is Stephenson her married name?"

"Oh. Of course." She hadn't thought of that.

Max probably knew Kate before she was married. Such a silly system, changing your name when you married. It made it so tricky to trace people.

Max walked faster. "I wonder... I knew a Kate when I worked in the bank in Bristol, just after I left university. Kate Mitchell was her name."

"Did you know her well?" Libby made an effort to sound relaxed.

"We went around together for a while. Nothing intense. It all fizzled out when I met my wife and we lost touch over the years. I haven't seen her since then."

"Well, she seems to know a lot about you." Libby caught her lower lip between her teeth, annoyed at the edge in her voice.

Max, deep in his own thoughts, seemed not to notice. He murmured, almost to himself, "I suppose my divorce is common knowledge, but how did she know about Debbie? We lived in London when she died."

Max had told Libby the sad story: he'd had a row with his teenage daughter, she'd flounced away, ridden her horse without a helmet, fallen and suffered a fatal head injury. At the time he'd been focused on making big money as a banker, and he'd let family relationships slip. After Debbie's death, he'd blamed himself and hit the whiskey bottle, hard. A messy divorce soon followed.

The knot in Libby's stomach tightened its grip. Kate Stephenson had certainly done her homework. Libby straightened her shoulders, tossed aside the leaf, and took Max's hand. "I imagine Kate's the kind of person who has her ear to the ground. Let's not worry about it. There's no need for you to do anything."

"I suppose not." Max sounded less than convinced.

Libby tried a change of subject. "Anyway, I want to concentrate on Liam Weston's death. We still know so little about him."

"That's why I brought you out here, today, to St Mary's church. I'm hoping the local rector will be able to tell us more." Max squeezed Libby's hand. "He's been at St Mary's for ten years or so. That's long enough to find out all about the local population."

"What did you say his name was?"

"John Canterbury."

Libby laughed. "That's a good name for a rector, especially one with ambition."

"The couple of times I've run into John, playing skittles in one of the local pubs, he's struck me as someone completely uninterested in moving up the hierarchy. We won't be seeing him inducted as Bishop of Bath and Wells any time soon. Oh, and here we are…"

The tiny church, attached by a stone wall to a couple of small thatched cottages, was distinguished by a spire that pointed heavenward. Libby glanced round. Another churchyard; her second in a couple of days. They walked the short distance to the heavy wooden door of the church and left the dogs outside, lying happily in the shade. Even Shipley seemed content to rest quietly, for once.

Max and Libby entered the cool, dark interior of the church. Tacked to a cork board on Libby's right were a dozen or so notices, some printed, several handwritten. A quick scan showed they were notices of events about to take place in the village. The local playgroup was due to meet on Tuesday mornings and Thursday afternoons. The cricket team was playing away next week in Devon, a bring-and-buy sale was due in a few days, and a Grand Summer Quiz was advertised for this evening, to be held in the church hall. An entry ticket entitled the holder to a free glass of wine or a soft drink.

Everything on the board suggested a calm, peaceful community, crime free, where organising an evening without falling foul of the licensing laws was a main concern. Could Liam's death, not two miles away, really be murder? Libby had doubts. Perhaps she'd been reading too much into a careless accident. She'd let the strange Papadopoulos couple spook her, and that unnerving experience in Kate Stephenson's house had left her nerves jangling. A dose of uncomplicated low-key Anglican religion would calm her twitchy nerves.

They walked into the body of the church, to be greeted by a small, round, smiling man wearing enormous glasses. The spectacles were held in place by two very large ears that stood out almost at right angles from his head. With an effort to avoid staring at these twin excrescences, Libby kept her eyes on the centre of the man's face as Max introduced her. "Libby, this is John Canterbury, the rector of this parish, and several others in the area."

The rector, exactly the kind of welcoming vicar Libby had hoped for, beamed. "How lovely to see you again, Max, though I haven't forgiven you for your part in that last skittles match. My team will be taking vengeance very soon. Now, I hope you didn't mind meeting me here. I just popped into the church to make sure everything was ready for the funeral later today. Mrs Banks, one of the most stalwart members of my congregation, I'm afraid, passed away last week. Almost ninety, so the event was not unexpected, but the loss will weaken our Sunday singing even more."

His mouth drooped comically, but the twinkle in his eyes remained. "I suppose you don't live around here, Mrs Forest, and better yet, sing?"

"Sorry. I'm from Exham. And not really a churchgoer, I'm afraid."

"Ah well, not to worry." The good humour was infectious. "We'll have to make do with our choir of six, and hope no more are called away to higher things. We could use some young boys and girls, really. Anthony Palmer's the only choir member still at school, and he's obliged to attend because his father's our churchwarden. Lovely voice, the child has. Quite beautiful, but a few months left before it breaks." He heaved a sigh. "Still, you didn't come here to talk about church music, I'm sure."

He straightened a pile of leaflets, handing one to Libby. "Here's a short history of the parish. You may find it interesting."

She tucked the leaflet into her bag and followed the rector out of the dim light in the church into bright June sunshine.

"Now, Max." The smiling vicar leaned against the ancient honey-coloured wall of the nearest cottage. "I live just up the lane. Not in this charming cottage, sadly. Mrs Banks' daughter has that pleasure. But if you come with me, I'm sure I can rustle up a can of tomato soup and some bread. Not much to offer a famous cook such as yourself, Mrs Forest, but perhaps it will stave off the worst of the afternoon's hunger pangs."

***

The rector lived in the small, modern bungalow on the edge of the village. He led Libby and Max inside. "My wife's at work, so you'll have to put up with me, I'm afraid. She's a pharmacist at the local hospital. Let's see what she's left for lunch."

Instead of the promised can of Heinz soup, John's wife had left plates of salmon and cucumber sandwiches and an apple pie, all tightly covered in cling film. The kitchen was clean and tidy, almost as neat as Libby's own, though without the industrial-scale oven and sink units. The rector removed a pile of books and papers from the scrubbed table in the dining room: a Bible, leaflets, and a couple of heavy reference books.

The rector noticed her interest. "Some fascinating information about old Somerset in these books. Glastonbury, of course, is so old it was mentioned in William the Conqueror's

Doomsday Book, as well as in this one about old religions."

Libby peered more closely: *A History of Ancient Somerset* and *The Golden Bough.* "There's so much to find out about the county's history," she said. "I've only been here a year or two, and I'm still learning."

Max chuckled. "All the old places seem to have present-day mysteries, as well as the old ones. Did you hear about the body on Glastonbury Tor, and the murder in Wells library?"

"Oh, yes. I've been following your adventures with admiration," the rector said. "So I'm not surprised you're interested in young Liam's story, Mrs Forest. I expect that's what you wanted to ask me about?"

Libby nodded and the rector continued, "Poor lad. I knew him well, of course. At least his parents went before him. There's nothing worse than burying your own child. Those are the worst funerals for the clergy, you know, because it's so hard to find the smallest crumb of comfort for the parents. It seems against the natural order of things for a child to go before his parents. Older people, now, they're another matter. When they've lived a happy life, they're often ready to pass on."

His round face beamed with goodwill that hinted he'd find just the right words to say to grieving relatives. He went on, "Liam was well liked around these parts, despite his hot temper, and he was a hard worker, I believe. Wanted to set up his own herd of cattle, learning everything he could from Mike Carmichael. He was like one of the family to Mike and Belinda, you know. There are only a couple of years in age between Liam and Tim, their son."

He offered Libby another sandwich. "To tell you the truth, I think Mike would almost rather have had Liam as his heir. Tim's always been a little…" He laid a finger on his mouth, as though trying to stop criticism pass his lips. "How can I put it, now? Young Tim can be a little too fond of going out with his mates and having a good time. I'm sure he'll settle down in time too. Most do."

Libby drained a coffee cup. "My son just married Sarah, Tim's sister."

The rector beamed, revealing large white teeth, so crowded they crossed one another, lending a certain goofy charm to his smile. "Now, she's a lovely girl, is Sarah. I always thought she'd end up with a local boy like Liam." He raised both hands in the air in an apologetic gesture. "So sorry, that came out wrong. No offence intended."

"None taken. I suppose most people round here end up marrying people they've grown up with?"

The rector smiled at Libby. "Ah, now, that used to happen a great deal. Of course, it's not just inbreeding that makes folk behave oddly. Dementia, now, is a big problem, these days. Old people lose their memories. Look what happened at your son's wedding, for example, about Lady Antonia's ring." He shook his head. "The poor woman's having a few problems, I'm afraid. We can't all keep as sharp as our recently departed Mrs Banks. She was on the ball, terrorising choirboys for every wrong note, until the day she died."

He chuckled. "Still, now, I've been rambling on. What was I saying?" He glanced around, eyes narrowed, as though searching for inspiration. "Oh yes. Children don't stay around here, like they used to. Wages are low, and it's easier to find work in the cities." He poured more coffee. "It's good to have new life in the area." He looked from Max to Libby, and she felt a blush start on her neck.

Max stepped in, bringing the conversation firmly back to Liam. "What can you tell us about the lad who died?"

The rector steepled his fingers and closed his eyes. "Not a churchgoer, I'm sorry to say. At least, only at Christmas and Easter, along with most people here." The grin returned. "Best attendance I ever have is when we bless the animals. Church is full of folk, those days, apart from the goats, sheep, and donkeys. Once, we even had a llama up from Barrow Farm over in that direction."

Libby asked, "How well did Tim and Liam get on? Were they friends?"

The rector let out a sharp bark of laughter. "Not them. Jealousy, you know."

Libby leaned forward. "Which way? Was Liam jealous of Tim, or the other way round?"

The rector leaned back, arms folded. "Tim resented the way his father relied on Liam. Now, don't get me wrong. A little bit of jealousy doesn't mean Tim would want to hurt Liam, but since Liam became Mike's right-hand man, Tim refused to have anything to do with farm business. He works in Minehead, these days, with a feed supplier."

He rose, his chair scraping awkwardly on the laminated floor, and began to stack dishes in the dishwasher. "Now, I'm afraid I have to get away and finish preparations for old Mrs Banks. Come and see me again soon, won't you? I'd love to hear about your adventures as our local sleuth."

CHAPTER TEN

Sultana cake

Libby spent the drive back to Exham thinking about the rector's words. No one yet knew if Liam was the victim of a murderer, or an accident. There was no evidence of foul play, but Libby was learning to trust her instincts. While the police checked for giveaway fibres from clothes, and tested blood samples, Libby kept wondering who might want Liam dead, and why.

So far, he seemed to be an ordinary, hard-working farm hand with no family and no obvious girlfriend. There had been no sign of a 'plus one' at the wedding. No one gained from his death.

What about hatred? "Max, what was it the rector said about Tim and Liam?"

" 'Tim resented the way his father relied on Liam.' That's what I remember." Max chuckled. "Are you thinking what I'm thinking? Maybe Tim hated Liam more than others realised. He'd even walked away from the family business out of jealousy."

Libby groaned. "And that business with the ring at the wedding. Tim could easily have set that up to incriminate Liam. Then, as that turned out to be a damp squib, he might have caused the accident."

"Wait a moment. Let's not get too far ahead. How could Tim arrange Liam's death?"

"In any number of ways." Libby counted ideas on her fingers. "Brake failure or tyre pressure, or some other damage to the tractor…"

"The police would notice that…"

"Poison?"

"Some unnoticeable poison from the Amazon rain forest? Come on, Libby, how likely is that."

She shrugged. He wasn't taking her seriously. "There are other untraceable poisons, you know." She let the silence hang a moment. "Anyway, my point is, Tim is definitely a suspect."

"I'll give you that," Max's hands gripped the wheel firmly, "but we need to keep open minds. We don't know of any other motive, yet. Let's keep looking. Meanwhile, is this afternoon the first of Shipley's retraining classes? Are you willing to take him? I know I'm his official owner, but he's your dog, really."

He sounded distant. Libby shifted in her seat. If it wasn't her imagination, a rift was growing between them. Max had been different this morning; unusually polite and thoughtful, letting Libby do most of the talking. Libby missed the robust teasing she'd grown used to hearing.

His attitude to Shipley had changed, too. Perhaps he was mentally sorting things into piles: sorting out which were his possessions and which belonged to Libby. Her fingers tightened on the seat belt. Those were not thought processes of someone contemplating marriage. Maybe Max was having second thoughts.

Libby stuck her jaw out. She wasn't going to lay herself open to rejection. If Max was losing interest in her, it was a good thing they'd never made any real commitment. They could carry on as business partners and Shipley could live with Libby.

She blinked hard and took a deep breath, forcing herself to concentrate on events in the Exmoor villages. She had a bad feeling about the people she'd met recently. Instinct again? Well, this time she wouldn't tell Max. She was perfectly capable of visiting the Papadopoulos couple alone. Shipley would protect her.

***

Shipley's snores reverberated in Libby's ears on the drive back to Exmoor. The hour-long obedience training had exhausted the poor animal, and he wasn't the only one. Libby's head spun from the effort of remembering the commands. It wasn't just the words that mattered, she'd learned. It was all about tone of voice and gesture. "We've both been back to school this afternoon, Shipley."

Shipley paused on his way into the Citroen, sniffing round the boot of the car. Inside, safe in a tin wrapped in layers of cardboard was a cake Libby had picked up from home. She had a plan to gain entry to the Papadopoulos house, and the cake was an important element. Who could resist sultana cake? "You can smell it, can't you?"

The dog's ability was amazing. No wonder the ex-policeman who ran the session was impressed. "That dog would have made a brilliant drug sniffer," he'd said.

Tanya had laughed. "Or mortuary dog. Isn't that what they call them? Dogs that can pick out a dead body from miles away?" She grinned at Libby. "You could do with one of those in your line of work, Libby."

"I'm hoping it won't be necessary for a while. Too many deaths have happened in the area already."

The dog slept in the back of the car while Libby enjoyed a little peace and quiet. As she passed the pub in the next village, she waved at the barmaid rearranging chairs in the sunshine, but her mood slipped as she drew nearer to Upper Compton.

Shipley woke, looked out of the window, lost interest, and scratched the back seat, as though trying to dig through to the boot of the car. Libby, suddenly nervous, wished she'd left the cake at home. The excuse she'd dreamed up for her visit seemed wafer-thin. Well, it was too late now. She'd have to go through with it.

Her skin tingled as she drew up on the gravel outside the Papadopoulos's house. Solidly built, it boasted a central front door and symmetrical windows that gazed out like blank eyes. Libby retrieved the cake and rehearsed the story she'd planned during the drive. It sounded ridiculous, now, but it was too late to turn back. The occupants must have heard her arrival.

Trying to look more confident than she felt, she strode up the path leading between overgrown beach hedges to the front door, Shipley following close at heel, just as he'd been taught today. Usually, he'd bound ahead, barking wildly and running rings around Libby. This dog training business had already made a difference.

At the front door, Libby swallowed hard and leaned on the bell push, listening to the distant jangle echo through the house. She pasted a warm smile on her face as Olivia Papadopoulos opened the door and spoke as cheerily as possible. "Hello. I don't know if you remember me."

The woman's eyebrows twitched and a tight smile dissected her face. "Of course, I remember you, Mrs Forest."

Libby moistened her lips, straightened her shoulders, and embarked on her story. "I know you're friendly with Belinda at the farm. You see, I made this cake for her. It's meant to be a surprise, but when I took it to the house just now there was no one there. I don't want to transport it all the way back to Exham, and I remembered the quiz this evening in St Mary's church hall. Mike had mentioned it to me, and the rector said everyone attended, so I thought I'd take a chance you were going and ask if I could possibly leave the cake with you, to pass on to Belinda tonight."

She came to a sudden halt. The gabbled story sounded hopelessly contrived.

"Then you'd better come in." Mrs Papadopoulos smiled. "Why, I'd be delighted to pass on your cake. Belinda's told me how brilliantly you cook. Mind you," she led Libby down a long, gloomy corridor, turning left into a conservatory, "I might be tempted to eat it myself. What kind of cake is it?"

This was going better than Libby had

dreamed. The woman was so welcoming she'd even waved Shipley into the house behind Libby. Perhaps Libby had been too quick to judge. Just because her husband was weird, with strange, hippie clothes and cold eyes, it didn't mean Olivia was scary. Libby had been imagining things, at the farm. Mike and Xavier had business to discuss, that was why they'd wanted Libby gone. She relaxed, cheered by her internal pep-talk. "Sultana."

"Oh my. My favourite." The woman heaved a loud sigh. "Never mind, I'll wait until the quiz. Perhaps Belinda will share."

The woman seemed inclined to chat. Libby gestured towards the woodland visible through the conservatory glass. "What a wonderful setting for your house."

"Yes, we're very lucky. It's just the place for our little meetings."

"Meetings?"

Olivia's eyebrow twitched. "Just a few friends, you know. We get together from time to time to share memories."

In the distance, music played. Olivia wore an odd expression. "That's my husband. We have a grand piano in the music room."

"How wonderful," Libby heard herself gush. "I recognise the music. Rachmaninov, isn't it?"

Olivia's smile grew broader. "So, you're a musician, Mrs Forest?"

"Not really…"

"Come, he won't mind us listening. This way."

Libby followed the woman up the curved staircase. It led in a perfect spiral to an upstairs landing. Mrs Papadopoulos took Libby's arm. "Come in. He'll be so pleased to play for you."

Her fingers were tight against Libby's flesh. "I need to go," Libby said, suddenly nervous. She stepped aside, shaking off the woman's fingers.

"Nonsense, my dear, you can spare a minute or two to enjoy the music." Olivia pushed open the heavy door to reveal her husband, half-hidden by a beautifully polished grand piano. "Look dear," she said. "Remember Mrs Forest? She's enjoying your music."

Xavier Papadopoulos stopped, hands resting motionless above the keys, and smiled at Libby. "I knew we would be seeing more of you, Mrs Forest. I'm never mistaken about people. Now, what can we do for you?"

"I was just-er-bringing a cake. For Belinda Carmichael. She's not at home." Libby's voice sounded thin in the large room. She spoke louder. "I hope you don't mind my dog being in here. He's rather excitable."

Giving the lie to her words, Shipley remained

motionless, nose in the air as if he smelled something no human could detect.

Olivia Papadopoulos laughed. "Dogs always behave beautifully around my husband. He has a gift for animals, you know. One of many."

Libby forced a smile. "Well, the music was certainly beautiful, but I need to be getting back now."

Olivia Papadopoulos took her arm again. Once more, the bony fingers gripped just a fraction too tightly. "It's been such a pleasure to have you with us. If you're free this evening, why not come to our quiz too, and give Belinda her cake in person. We could use another team member. Liam Weston was in our team, poor boy, and we miss him dreadfully. Such a sad death."

Libby's rapid increase in heart rate warned her to refuse the invitation. This pair gave her the creeps. She wanted to get out of the house, drive away, and never come back, but the possibility of finding out more about Liam was too good to turn down. That was, after all, why she'd trekked out to Exmoor in the first place.

At least, she'd be able to spend a minute or two alone with Belinda. The two women hadn't met since the wedding, and Belinda seemed never to answer a phone. The quiz night might be Libby's best opportunity to get to the bottom of

Belinda's problem.

**

Libby hoped to spend a few moments alone with Belinda before the evening's entertainment began, but Mike was already seated with the Papadopoulos couple and, to Libby's dismay, there was no sign of his wife. Olivia rose and approached Libby. "Such a shame." She sounded breathless. "Belinda came home from her shopping trip today, with a dreadful cold, so Mike sent her to bed. Such good luck you've joined us. Mike can take your cake home later."

Libby couldn't care less about the wretched cake. She wanted to see Belinda. Hadn't the woman been on a shopping trip when Libby visited the farm? Did the woman do nothing but shop?

Thinking hard, Libby subsided into her seat at a table spread with sheets of paper and a pile of pens. She nibbled squares of cheese. Perhaps Belinda regretted mentioning her money worries when they spoke at the wedding. She'd been avoiding Libby ever since.

The rector scurried round, settling people in their seats, sorting lone arrivals into teams, and pouring wine. There were empty chairs at Libby's table, but when someone from the next table claimed them, Xavier Papadopoulos shook his head. "So sorry, we're waiting for the rest of our team."

Libby watched the door. At the last moment, just as the rector tapped a spoon against a glass to call for quiet, the latecomers arrived. As Max entered, Kate Stephenson leaning on his arm, Libby's breath stuck in her throat. "What are you doing here?" she hissed. "You might have told me."

"You didn't tell me you were coming, either."

Libby bit back angry words. He was right. Under cover of the rector's voice, as he gave instructions for the quiz, she muttered, "OK. But why are you here?"

"Kate invited me. Remember? We knew each other years ago." Libby had carried Kate's message herself. "Give my regards to Max," Kate had said, pearly teeth gleaming.

There was no time for further talk, for the quiz had begun. As the evening progressed, Libby grew hotter and more annoyed, while Max spent the evening ignoring her, leaning much too close to Kate Stephenson. The alternative therapist knew almost all the answers, from the names of obscure capital cities to the top forty pop tunes of the 1980s.

For some reason, Libby could hardly remember her own name, never mind the names of five chemical elements beginning with vowels. The more she tried to think, the less she remembered. She thought she might explode when she caught sight of Xavier Papadopoulos watching her, a patronising smile across his face, as she gave yet another wrong answer to a geography question. How was she supposed to know the names of land-locked African countries, anyway?

The final straw came at the end of the evening. Libby's team came second, but Kate won a prize for the best individual performance.

CHAPTER ELEVEN

Croissants

Libby was first to arrive at the bakery next morning, determined to put Belinda and the Papadopoulos couple out of her mind. She wished she could so easily forget the way Max had looked at Kate. As she unlocked the shop, switched on the oven and mixed flour with yeast and water, her head swam with images of the alternative therapist, all smiles, head close to Max's as they argued whether or not Botswana was on the coast of Africa. Libby took out her anger on a mound of dough.

The front-door bell jangled and Mandy burst into the shop. "Have you seen it?"

"Seen what?" Libby thumped harder.

"They've started work on the new shop. You know, where Leather Heaven used to be? Guess who's bought it?" The small, independent shoe shop had been forced out of business during the recession and the premises had passed through several pairs of hands since.

An invisible cloud of doom seemed to gather over Libby's head. "Terence Marchant?"

Mandy nodded. "I just saw Peter. He couldn't wait to give me the news. Smug little…" With a show of huge self-control, she fell silent.

"Quite." Libby squeezed dough between her fingers. "I suppose we knew it would happen sometime." Viciously, she chopped the dough into equal portions and tossed each into an oiled metal bowl.

"What can we do? If Frank's bakery closes, I'll be out of work and I won't get a chance to finish my apprenticeship." Mandy was breathing hard.

Libby forced a smile. "Don't worry. We have plenty of outlets for the chocolates, thanks mainly to your business flair, so we'll keep going even if the worst happens. Poor Frank, though. The new shop's likely to dent his profits, and he hasn't seemed really well since that business with the poisoned cyclists."

Mandy said, "That's an idea. I suppose poisoning the competition's out of the question?"

Before Libby could answer, the morning's first customers arrived, full of gossip about the new shop. "I hear they'll be serving those French crossings," old Mrs Blandish announced, handing over a pile of coppers in payment for her weekly order of a small split tin and half a dozen currant

113

buns.

"Croissants?" Mandy suggested.

The old lady shrugged. "Some such. Can't get my tongue round these foreign words." She winked at Libby. "You'd better check that money. Never was much good at sums," she said, as she did every time.

Libby counted coins into the till, sucking in her cheeks to keep her face straight. "Perfect as always." She avoided Mandy's eye. Like many of the town's oldest citizens, widowed Mrs Blandish rarely left Exham on Sea except for an annual trip to Birmingham to stay with her daughter. A farmer's wife all her married life, she'd certainly never had leisure to cross the Channel for a taste of real French croissants. Perhaps Terence Marchant's raid on Frank's customers would fail, as they stuck to their old ways.

***

Later that day, Libby's kitchen rang with the noise of chocolate grinders and food processors. She emptied smooth, tempered chocolate into piping bags and began to fill paper cases. Mandy sat on the other side of the room, fingers flying over a computer keyboard as she recorded weights, volumes, and notes about the ingredients.

"I gave this batch an extra two minutes," Libby called. "I think perhaps the beans were less ripe than the last ones. Fingers crossed I got it right."

Mandy tapped into the machine. "Me too, Mrs F. That was one expensive batch."

"It puts the unit price up quite a bit," Libby admitted, "but with luck, it'll improve the quality."

"Enough for us to call it a premier range?"

Libby looked up again, surprised. "Good idea. I hadn't thought of that." She paused, impatient to reveal the surprise she had in store for her apprentice. "Mandy, I've got something for you." She peeled off her gloves, opened a drawer, and took out a set of keys, dangling them in front of Mandy. "Here."

Mandy leapt to her feet. "You mean…"

"Don't get too excited. It's just an old banger, but it should get you around the countryside."

Mandy grabbed the keys, and dashed outside. "Where is it?"

Libby giggled. "It's hidden round the corner. I wanted it to be a surprise."

She followed Mandy down the street. "There." She pointed at a bright yellow car. "It's five years old, but it's only done 20,000 miles. Go on, try it out. It belongs to the business, officially, but you can hang onto it."

Mandy, breathless with excitement, drove away with a flourish. The house seemed suddenly quiet. Libby piled used bowls in the dishwasher, suddenly lonely. There was plenty more work to do, but she'd lost her enthusiasm.

She trudged upstairs to the bathroom, where the airing cupboard door was ajar. A pair of green eyes gleamed in the depths of the cupboard. Libby addressed her marmalade cat. "At least you're still here with me, Fuzzy." The cat opened her eyes, glanced at her mistress, and turned her back. Libby sighed. "You're such good company."

Shipley appeared from behind her back and Fuzzy hissed. Libby diverted the dog down the stairs and out into the garden.

Back in the kitchen, she settled in Mandy's chair and looked at the business records. An hour later, she raised her head and rubbed her eyes. The business was fine. She should be excited, but despite her best attempts she couldn't raise more than a small smile. Mandy was doing a lot of the heavy lifting. The records showed increased sales, not only to Jumbles, their main outlet in Bath, but also to other department stores in Bristol and even Exeter. Three small shops in Taunton were stocking Mrs Forest Chocolates.

Libby had to face it. Mandy was a far better businesswoman than she would ever be. She'd earned the car.

As Libby finished adding columns of figures, her phone rang. Her heart lurched as she glanced at the display screen. Why was Robert phoning from his honeymoon?

"Mum?" The panicked voice was almost unrecognisable. "It's Sarah. She's gone."

CHAPTER TWELVE

Sarah

"Where are you?" Libby managed to keep her voice calm.

"I'm in the hotel. Mum, I don't know what to do."

Libby guessed he was pacing, unable to settle. "Sit down, breathe out, and tell me what happened."

"Sarah and I had a row, yesterday. It wasn't anything really, just one of those stupid arguments about which restaurant to choose. I wanted to eat in the hotel and she wanted to go somewhere new."

"That doesn't sound too serious. Did she drive off in a huff, or something?"

"No, nothing like that. We made it up. I took her out to the hotel she wanted, though I don't know why she was so keen to go there. It wasn't as nice as this place."

Libby forced herself to be patient. "So when did she disappear?"

"We finished our steaks and the waitress brought the dessert menu. Sarah can't resist a dessert. She's a Pavlova and chocolate tart kind of a girl, but before she'd even ordered, she went to the ladies and didn't come back."

"You mean, she left the restaurant?"

"She took the car. I had to get a taxi."

At least, if she'd taken the car, it was Sarah's choice to leave. She hadn't been abducted. Libby had been letting her imagination run away. She opened her mouth to ask questions, but closed it again. She'd never find the truth through the telephone. Instead, she said, "I'm on my way. Don't move until I arrive."

***

The hotel was a large, five star affair on the Devon and Somerset border overlooking the sea. It was hardly any distance from Exham as the crow flew, but the winding roads of rural Somerset tripled the length of the journey. Stuck behind a tractor on the steep incline from Porlock, Libby gripped the wheel with white knuckles.

She should have asked Max to lend her the Land Rover, but they hadn't spoken since the quiz. She'd been too annoyed about Kate Stephenson. The car chugged slowly up the hill and she feared the engine was about to give up the attempt. "Hurry up," she muttered through clenched teeth.

As the vehicle coughed its way between the tall ivy-covered walls leading to the hotel, Libby's stomach turned over as she caught sight of her son, waving from the imposing entrance. She left the car on the gravel drive. She'd argue with the hotel management later, if necessary.

Robert's face was puffy and pink. He'd looked like that as a little boy, falling over, scraping his hands and knees, and then trying not to cry. Usually undemonstrative, he wrapped his arms round his mother in a giant bear hug. "I'm so glad you're here. I just didn't know what to do."

Libby led him into the lounge and ordered cups of tea, judging that to be more calming than coffee. He was already hyped up.

At last, stammering and hiccuping, he told Libby the story. He'd waited in the restaurant, choosing dessert, relieved Sarah had forgotten their quarrel. He'd topped up her glass and settled back, looking round the room. "After she'd been gone about a quarter of an hour, I thought it was part of some practical joke," he said. "You know how the lads were teasing, saying they knew where we were going for the honeymoon. I thought they might have set me up, but the place was full of couples and I didn't recognise anyone."

He tried to laugh and Libby thought her heart would break as he screwed his knuckles into his eyes. "Eventually, I asked one of the waitresses to go into the ladies to check for Sarah."

"But she wasn't there?"

"She'd disappeared."

Libby said, "Did you call the police?"

"They'll say she left of her own accord. After all, she is an adult, but she isn't answering her phone, and she always has it with her."

"Maybe the battery's run out?"

Robert gave a painful laugh. "You know Sarah. She's too efficient to let that happen."

It was true. Libby had often envied Sarah's organisational abilities. "It's probably time to contact the police, now she's been away all night."

Robert shrugged. "They won't do anything."

"Not at first" Libby bit off the words. She'd been about to point out the police would be interested once Sarah had been missing for a few days. "Let's get home to Exham. You should go to the farm and tell Sarah's parents while I talk to Max."

***

Max looked hurt. His first words took Libby by surprise. "Why did you go rushing off to

Devon without telling me? Maybe I could have helped."

She clicked her tongue. "I can look after myself, you know." She had no time to worry about his feelings. "Robert's beside himself with worry, and I need to concentrate. What could Sarah have been doing, running away without telling him? They haven't been married a week, yet."

Max sighed. "Honeymoon quarrels? They're common enough. The happy couple spend a fortune on the ideal wedding, with so many details they're exhausted by the time it happens. They imagine a perfect day, a honeymoon like a holiday advertisement and never a cross word, until reality kicks in. Thousands of couples split up in the first year of marriage."

Libby frowned. "Even if that's true, this is more than a honeymoon spat. Sarah knows Robert will be beside himself with worry and she'd contact him if she could. I think we should talk to Joe, even if we keep it unofficial, to see what he thinks. After all, having a police officer in the family should give us a few advantages, don't you think?"

Libby winced at Max's mixed expression of amusement and irritation. She was giving out mixed messages which was unfair, although they accurately represented the confusion in her head. She'd work out whether she wanted to be part of Max's family later. "Please talk to Joe."

Max held up his hands. "I give in. I'll text him, see if he can come round once he's off duty. He's busy on Liam's case at the moment, and that's more important than Sarah driving off in a huff. At the moment, at least."

As he texted, Libby pondered aloud. "It's out of character for Sarah. She's always so sensible and thoughtful. She's brought Robert right out of his shell. Since she came into his life, he's sent me lovely presents on Mother's Day and hasn't forgotten my birthday once. She's too kind to let Robert worry, even if she's angry with him." She touched Max's hand. "You don't think something dreadful could have happened to her, do you?"

Max smiled, and the tension between them disappeared. "Let's not rush ahead, imagining the worst. One step at a time. Logic and good sense are your specialties, Lib, so keep a cool head. We'll work it out."

CHAPTER THIRTEEN

Belinda

While Max phoned his son, Libby watched Shipley exploring every inch of the garden, snuffling behind shrubs and following the trail of night visitors from the kitchen window. Bear leaned against her legs, his eyes on the younger dog, like a wise teacher minding an overexcited pupil.

Max followed them outside, dropping the phone in his pocket. "Joe agrees there's little the police can do until Sarah's been missing a while. Do her parents know she's missing?"

"Robert's already at the farm. He dropped me home and took my car." Her son's lanky body hunched over the steering wheel of Libby's tiny car would have made her laugh under less tense circumstances.

"Let's get over there." Max ushered the dogs into the Land Rover, brushing dried mud from the seats. "If Shipley's as clever as you say, maybe we could teach him to work a vacuum cleaner."

Normally, it would have been a joy to ride

through the countryside on such a day, with the mid-June sun shining, but not yet hot enough to bake the soil or dull the green of the grass verges. As they drew near Handiwater, the Carmichaels' farm, Libby's spirits plummeted further. Last time she'd visited, Mike's strange behaviour had unnerved her, and the Papadopoulos couple had set her teeth on edge, but those minor irritations paled to nothing compared to her dread of what she might find today. Belinda, Sarah's mother, would be beside herself with worry.

Mike was at the table, rocking gently and staring into space. A slice of toast lay, neglected, on a plate. Robert whispered, "I can't get any sense out of him, since I told him Sarah's missing. He's hardly hearing me."

Max laid a hand on Mike's shoulder. Mike. Come on, man. Let's find out what's going on."

Mike's eyes seemed out of focus. "What? What did you say?"

Libby sat on the opposite side of the table, leaning across to touch Mike's hand. "Where's Belinda?"

He heaved a long, heavy sigh. "Gone."

"Gone? Gone where? When?"

"A few days ago."

Libby and Max shared a startled look. Max said, "You mean, she was already missing when you were at the quiz?"

The farmer shrugged. "I thought she'd be back by now. But if Sarah's gone, too…" He left the end of the sentence hanging in the air.

Max walked round the table, pulled up a chair, and sat next to Libby. "I think you'd better tell us what's going on."

Mike was silent for a long time, until Libby's urge to give him a good shake became almost overwhelming. At last, Mike seemed to rouse himself from his thoughts. "She's been acting funny lately. We've always had the odd argument. Well, you do when you've been married awhile. She has a temper on her, does Belinda. A firecracker, that's what Sarah calls her."

Libby felt Robert stiffen at the mention of his new wife's name, but Mike kept talking. "She's often walked out the door, saying she won't return. Always comes back, though."

Libby put in, "How long does she stay away for?"

"That's the thing, you see. Never more than twenty-four hours before, no matter how angry she's been."

Robert stood up, his face pale. "But now, she and Sarah are both missing." He pressed a hand to his mouth. "Something terrible must have happened."

He looked from Max to Libby, eyes wide, his breathing ragged. "What are we going to do? How are we going to find them?" He took a step towards the door.

"Wait." Max's voice cut in. "We'll find them, for sure, but we need a plan, or else we'll rush around like headless chickens."

At that moment, the door flew open and Sarah's brother, Tim, burst in. "I came as fast as I could."

***

Tim's appearance in the farmhouse, looking as pale and distraught as his father, sent the tension levels in the room sky high. Libby put aside her suspicions over Tim's involvement in Liam's death, making a mental note to follow that up later. Meanwhile, his concern for his sister and mother was obvious in his strained face and staring eyes.

Determined to be practical, Libby said, "The first thing is to go through Belinda's papers." Robert interrupted. "What do you know about all this, Tim?"

Tim squared up to him. "Are you accusing me?"

Robert's chin jutted. "Seems to me, whenever

you're around, there's trouble."

Tim, face brick-red and furious, clenched both hands. "At least I haven't lost my wife less than a week after the wedding."

Robert swung a right towards Tim's face. Max intercepted, grabbing Robert's wrist and twisting it behind his back. Mike, roused from turpitude by the fight, jumped up, snatched at Tim and pinioned his son's arms, with the easy strength of a man who spent his life heaving bales of hay.

Libby, hands on hips, almost as angry as the two young men, raised her voice. "Can't you concentrate on what's important? Does it always have to be a competition with you boys?"

Mike changed his grip on Tim, giving his son a shove that sent him reeling back to crash into a chair. It teetered on two legs before clattering to the floor. "What would your mother say?" Mike snarled.

Tim regained his balance and brushed his jacket, his face mutinous. "He started it."

As Libby stifled a sudden, inappropriate urge to giggle, Max released Robert and sighed. "What are you, teenagers?"

Robert, avoiding his mother's eyes, subsided into a chair and leaned his elbows on the table, resting his head in his hands.

His father raised his voice. "Tim, sit down,

shut up for once in your life, and listen." Tim slouched towards the table and obeyed, curling a lip at the top of Robert's head.

Mike, apparently stirred back to life by the testosterone in the room, laid both hands on the table. "Now, if you two can stop behaving like ten-year-olds for a while, Mrs Forest was about to make suggestions. And before you argue," he forestalled Tim, who was rising from his seat, "Mrs Forest and Mr Ramshore are the experts. You listen to what they have to say or you'll leave my house. Got it?"

Libby took the sullen silence for agreement. "I was suggesting we go through any papers that Belinda might have in the house, to see if there are any clues as to where she might have gone."

Tim heaved himself to his feet. "I'll have a look through her desk."

Max caught Libby's eye, raised one eyebrow a millimetre, and suggested, "It might be better for Libby to look through Belinda's things. You know, they're both women. I'm sure Belinda would rather have it that way."

Libby had to admire Max's guile. She wanted to get to Belinda's papers before Tim had a chance, for he was still a suspect, and Max had hit on exactly the best way to make that happen. Men were so nervous about 'women's things'. What did they think they were going to find? It was a clever move.

Tim shrugged. "If you think you can find things quicker. I guess working as a private eye teaches you how to pry into other people's lives."

Libby groaned as her son, hands balled into fists, scraped his chair back. She held up a hand. "Don't start again."

Max said, "Tim and Robert, you make lists of Sarah's friends. Tim, you're likely to know her oldest friends while Robert identifies people she sees regularly. With any luck we'll end up with a full list." He turned to Mike. "Maybe you could do the same for Belinda? As soon as we've got the names, we can see if they know anything useful."

CHAPTER FOURTEEN

Pathway

Libby sat at Belinda's desk, situated in the corner of the tiny room used as a farm office. Three large filing cabinets stood in a row along one wall, each neatly labelled. "EU subsidies," she read aloud. "Milk 2000 to 2005," and, "milk 2005 to 2010". Deciding to ignore business documents and look for personal information first, Libby pulled open the top drawer of the desk. It was full of neatly arranged boxes of paper clips, Post-it® notes, staplers, scissors, and rulers. The second drawer was more interesting, containing a haphazard pile of documents. Libby lifted them out, elbowed aside the keyboard on the desktop, and began to work methodically through the pile.

Most of the papers were letters received in the past few weeks. It seemed this drawer was used as an inbox, which meant the third drawer was probably an outbox. To test the theory, Libby pulled open the third drawer. It was half empty. Belinda clearly used a computer in preference to pen and paper. Returning to the second drawer, Libby flipped through the first few layers of documents.

Leaflets and government instructions made up most of the correspondence. She found a couple of 'reply to wedding invitation' cards, both offering apologies from friends unable to attend Sarah's wedding. Libby recalled Sarah's excitement about her wedding day and offered up a brief prayer that the young woman had come to no harm. Robert's heart would be broken if anything happened to his new wife.

She finished reading the letters in the pile, finding nothing of interest, dumped them back in the drawer, flipped the drawer shut, and turned to the computer.

After the usual wait while the machine slowly woke, a dialogue box appeared requesting a password. Libby was about to return to the kitchen to ask Mike, when her eye was caught by a sticky note attached to the desk lamp. It seemed Belinda, like most people, had difficulty remembering passwords.

Libby used to keep her own next to the computer, until Max and Mandy joined forces and insisted she set up a spreadsheet with all the passwords she needed, saving it under yet another password. She'd complained, "What if I forget that one?"

Max had laughed. "I'll put it in my list. And you put mine in yours. So long as at least one of us manages to remember our password, we'll be all right."

With an effort, Libby swallowed the lump in her throat. He'd probably be sharing passwords with Kate Stephenson, soon. Startled by her own thoughts, Libby dropped the note. It was jealousy, pure and simple, that was making her angry with Max.

She shook her head. "Not now," she muttered, and entered the combination of numbers and letters. It worked. She could now access Belinda's programs. Email. That was the first place to look.

She crossed her fingers, hoping Belinda would not have bothered with more passwords, and sure enough, the inbox opened at the first click. Libby scanned the list of senders. Most of the traffic dealt with arrangements for Sarah's wedding and lunches with friends. There was an exchange with Sarah, discussing the colour of the bridesmaids' dresses, and a note to Belinda's aunt, asking whether she needed help to get to the wedding. "And, thank you for lending us your jewellery. Sarah would love to wear the pearls," it ended. They had been the 'something old' worn by the bride.

One name in the senders' list caught Libby's attention. The sender was X. "Xavier?" she wondered aloud.

With one click, she opened the email. "Remember not to deviate from the Pathway."

Libby checked the date. The email had arrived three days ago, the day Belinda disappeared. She printed out the email and set it on one side, her pulse racing, and scanned the rest of the email, but found nothing more from X. She searched with the word Path and Pathway, excited to discover two items. To her disgust, they contained nothing more threatening than a lawn mower advertisement and a reference to paving stones. Belinda, it seemed, was a keen gardener.

Max's eyes opened wide when she showed him the email. "If that's not a threat, then I'm a Dutchman."

Libby waved the sheet of paper at Mike. "Is this from Xavier Papadopoulos?"

The farmer's cheek twitched. "I don't know. I never use the computer – can't abide staring at a screen. I leave all that to Liam. He prints out emails that come for me and I tell him how to respond. I don't know anything about Belinda's account. No idea who she's been talking to."

He turned away and reached for the kettle. His

hand shook so that he could hardly lift it. Max said, "Don't you think it's time you came clean with us? I think you know more than you're letting on about your wife's disappearance. What's going on?"

The farmer looked from Libby to Max, groaned, and sank into the nearest chair. "I can't. I can't tell you anything."

Max said, "In that case, it's time we called in the police."

Tim and his father spoke together. "No!"

Tim licked his lips. "Come on, Dad. I guess it's time to explain."

***

Mike leaned his elbows on the table, head between his hands, face hidden. "Belinda hasn't been… Well, she hasn't been herself for a long time. It all started when her mother died. Two years ago, that was. They'd always been close and Belinda took it very hard. She wouldn't talk to me about it, but the church helped. She started going to church of a Sunday."

The sound he uttered lay midway between a laugh and a moan. "We'd never really been churchgoers. We were baptised, of course. Everyone was in those days, and we went to

Sunday School. Mostly to give our parents a bit of peace at the weekend, I reckon."

He made a ghastly attempt at a smile. "We hadn't set foot in the church for years, but the rector came round about her mother's funeral, and he was very kind to Belinda. He came back a few times, to talk about her mother, and Belinda went to church once or twice. She liked it there. Said they were friendly. She wanted me to go too, but I can't abide all that singing and kneeling. Anyway, after a while, it got to be a habit and she was going every Sunday."

Libby, impatient, longed to hurry him, but she knew Mike needed to take his time. She forced herself to speak quietly. "Where does Xavier Papadopoulos come in?"

"I'm getting to that. Even though she kept going to church, Belinda was unhappy. I suppose you could say she was depressed. She could hardly get out of bed in the morning, and that wasn't like her. Even in the spring, when we were lambing, she wouldn't go into the fields. Until then, it was her favourite job. She used to stay out overnight, helping the ewes."

Tim joined in, with an awkward laugh. "Mum was the best for a difficult lambing. She has tiny hands, you see."

The nerve in Mike's cheek twitched. "Going to

church helped a bit. She got friendly with some of the folks there, meeting them for coffee and so on. Then, one day, she met Olivia Papadopoulos. You met her, remember, that day you visited?"

"Of course. She and her husband didn't seem pleased to find me here."

Mike fidgeted, rubbing his leg. "He'd come to... I mean, he was on business." He shot a glance at Libby, eyes narrowed, and looked away again. "Not one to chat, Xavier Papadopoulos. He can be a bit sharp, but I owe him a lot. Belinda's recovery was his doing."

"Really?" Libby found that difficult to believe. Mike's restlessness suggested he was holding something back. Libby glanced at Max for confirmation, and he returned the smallest nod.

"Olivia invited Belinda to their house one evening. They run these groups, you see, of bereaved people, where they all get together and, well, talk, I suppose. It seems to help. It wouldn't do for me but it worked a treat for Belinda." Libby guessed that a stoic farmer like Mike would run a mile from any talking therapy.

"Is this group the Pathway in the email?"

He wrinkled his nose. "That's what they called it. The Pathway to Health."

Max joined the conversation. "Have you been to any of these meetings, Mike?"

The farmer lurched to his feet, grabbed empty coffee cups from the table and piled them in the sink. "Belinda preferred to go alone, and I didn't mind. It was good to have the old Belinda back again." He dropped a cup. It shattered, the sharp crack reverberating round the kitchen. He made no attempt to pick up the pieces.

He swung round, worry etched on the lines across his forehead and round his mouth. "Just recently, she's been busy with the wedding and I thought she was back to her old self. She wasn't going to the Pathway meetings so often, being busy on the farm, you see. She even helped with the lambs again." A brief smile lit his face. "She had three orphans in the kitchen at one time, giving them the bottle all through the day and night."

Mike ran his hand over the back of his head, rubbing the hair until sparse strands stood on end. "Olivia came over to talk to her one day. I was out in the fields, so I don't know what she said to my wife, but Belinda was crying when I got back. In floods of tears, as bad as when her mother died. She wouldn't tell me what was wrong, just that she didn't want to go back to those meetings. I suppose they fell out. That's what happens in these groups. Bickering, you know."

Libby nodded. She'd seen plenty of squabbles

at the Exham History Society, and on her visits to the Knitters' Guild. The atmosphere could be electric. If only she'd been a fly on the wall when Olivia Papadopoulos fell out with Belinda.

Tired of trying to guess what Mike was holding back, Libby strode across the room and confronted him. "Be honest, Mike. Why were the Papadopoulos couple here, that day I met them. Was it really business?"

Mike looked straight at Libby, at last. "They came about Belinda. They said she'd agreed to go to a Pathway meeting the day after the wedding, but hadn't turned up. I told them she'd been tired, but that wasn't the truth. She hadn't wanted to go. I could tell something had upset her, and she didn't want anything more to do with them. She told me she was going to the shops instead. She didn't expect them to come round to the farm."

He flattened his hair with one hand. "After you'd gone, I told Xavier and Olivia to stop coming around. If Belinda didn't want to go to their group any more, she didn't have to. They gave me a load of bull about letting down the other group members and I said I'd pass the messages on to Belinda. But she never came home."

Max said, "So, she disappeared and Xavier Papadopoulos and his wife had no idea where she went?" He was rubbing a finger along his upper lip, a gesture he used when deep in thought. "Or was that the impression they wanted to give?"

Max didn't trust the strange couple any more than Libby did. The thought was comforting. She said, "I think we should pay a visit to the Papadopoulos couple. It sounds as though they were putting pressure on Belinda to keep within the group. Like some sort of cult. It sounds a bit sinister."

"I didn't know about any threatening email until today," Mike admitted. "Do you think that's why she disappeared?"

Max shrugged into his coat. "It's time we found out. Mike, you stay here in case Belinda or Sarah turn up. Robert and Tim, if you've finished those lists, get on your phones and see what you can find out about this group. What did you say it's called, Mike?"

Mike frowned, biting his lip. "The Pathway to Health."

"Meanwhile, Libby and I will visit Mr and Mrs Papadopoulos."

CHAPTER FIFTEEN

Meeting

"I could kick myself," Libby said, as the car sped away from the farm. "I've already been to their house and talked to the Papadopoulos pair, but I didn't get anything sensible from them." She told Max about her previous visit. Her voice rose. "In fact, that's why I was at the quiz."

She cleared her throat. Now wasn't the time to quarrel about Max's fawning over Kate Stephenson. "I thought Belinda would be there, but she didn't show up, although Olivia Papadopoulos behaved as though she expected her. Was she just pretending? I'm beginning to think that couple know a great deal about the disappearance of Belinda and Sarah. Xavier's always in the picture, even at the wedding. I'm sure he was the reason Belinda backed away from me. Then, they both popped up at Mike's farm and spooked him, and now there's evidence they were bullying Belinda. They're right at the top of my current list of suspects."

"Before we do too much guesswork, let's see if there's a good reason for Belinda and Sarah to run away. Maybe mother and daughter have gone off somewhere on their own. Belinda could be having some sort of breakdown, and Sarah's looking after her."

Libby snorted. "That's not likely. Sarah was on her honeymoon, for heaven's sake. You don't leave your new husband just after the wedding, to look after your mother. According to Robert, it was just a lover's spat."

Max's eyes stayed on the road. It was difficult to read his face. "Are you sure Robert's—well, I'll speak frankly. Is Robert telling the whole truth?"

Libby felt a chill at the base of her spine. How dare Max accuse her son? Her voice was cold. "What are you trying to say? You can't think Robert…"

"I'm just looking at the facts, as if he were any other young husband, having a row with his new wife."

Libby shifted in her seat to put more space between Max and herself. She heard the ice in her own voice. "If you're suggesting Robert had anything to do with Sarah's disappearance, you're mistaken. And why would he want to do anything to her mother?"

Max was soothing. "I'm sure Robert has

nothing to hide."

Libby could have hit him. "Don't try to placate me, as though I'm a stranger. I'm perfectly aware he'll be under police suspicion if Sarah isn't found soon, but I would think you'd trust him. He's my son."

She stared towards the hedge, where the branches loomed close enough to scratch the car. Max's hand touched her knee, but she pushed it away. How dare he suspect Robert? A tiny throb of anxiety started up at the back of her head. Trevor was the boy's father, and look at how he'd behaved. Like father, like son?

She closed her eyes. Pictures of Robert as a little boy filled her head. There was the day Ali, his little sister, broke his train set. He'd taken an hour to write a letter to Santa, tongue poking from the corner of his mouth, and he was too excited to sleep on Christmas Eve. Ali trod on his precious train and the funnel broke, but even then, Robert stayed calm.

Libby couldn't remember a single time before today that Robert had lost control of his temper. Relieved, she let out a puff of pent-up breath. "Robert is one of the gentlest, kindest people I know and I'm proud to be his mother. Tim pushed him too far, today. Robert wouldn't hurt a fly."

Max navigated a pothole that covered most of the lane. "I believe you. Anyway, there's no reason to suppose anything's happened to either Sarah or her mother. Until we know why they've disappeared, let's not quarrel about the suspects." He turned a corner and the house came into view. "Here we are. Maybe we'll find some answers now."

Just as before, when Libby had arrived with the cake, the front door was open before they had a chance to ring the bell. Libby muttered, "It's almost as though Olivia Papadopoulos spends all day sitting by the window, waiting for visitors."

"Why, Mrs Forest, how lovely to see you again." Olivia waved them into the house, a broad smile failing to reach her eyes. "And this must be Mr Ramshore. Of course, we've heard all about you from Mandy."

Libby stifled a gasp. "Mandy?"

The woman's eyes glittered. "She came to a meeting with our friend, Kate." Libby felt a familiar chill at the base of her spine, at the thought of Mandy being pulled into the orbit of the sinister Papadopoulos couple.

Olivia took her arm. "Come through. It's such a beautiful day, let's drink coffee in the conservatory. It's one of my favourite places."

Libby's thoughts raced. Why had Kate brought

Mandy here? Her stomach churned. Olivia did not appear to notice her silence, for Max kept up a calm flow of conversation. "I expect you know Belinda hasn't been home for a while. Mike, her husband, is getting anxious." He didn't mention Sarah's disappearance. "We wanted to talk to you because Belinda often comes to your groups."

Olivia waved Libby to a wicker chair facing the garden. As she sat, the sun shone full in her eyes and she shifted, uncomfortable, as though under a spotlight. Olivia poured coffee and offered cream and sugar. "I'm afraid Belinda's enthusiasm for our little group has waned recently." She gave a theatrical sigh. "It happens, I'm afraid. Some people take what they need from our gatherings and then leave. Others, of course, stay to help newcomers who need support."

Max smiled and sipped coffee. "We'd like to know more about the group."

Olivia's eyes narrowed, her face suddenly sharp, reminding Libby of a fox. "Tell me, Mr Ramshore, are you here as Belinda's friend or in some official capacity? I know you work with the police." She held up a hand, a ring on every finger, the painted nails long, like claws. "We have nothing to hide, but I think honesty's always best, don't you?"

Libby turned her head from side to side, trying

145

to avoid the sun. "My son's married to Belinda's daughter, Sarah, who also disappeared yesterday. As you can imagine, he's beside himself with worry. I'm here as a mother. Max and I are not being paid to investigate Belinda and Sarah's disappearance." They were being paid to investigate Liam's death, but Libby chose not to mention that. As yet, there seemed no link between the two, but she refused to believe a suspicious death and two mysterious disappearances were unconnected.

Olivia shook her head. "Ah. I was never blessed with children. It's my tragedy. Such trials brought me through tribulation to follow the Pathway to Health. My husband has many remarkable qualities as you know, Mrs Forest. One of those is his gift as a healer."

The door opened. Olivia rose to her feet. "And here he is. Sandy, you remember Libby Forest."

"My dear." Xavier Papadopoulos acknowledged Libby with a cold stare and a brief nod, but spoke to his wife. "Have you forgotten? Our meeting begins in two minutes." Olivia moved towards the door, patches of pink on her cheeks.

Her husband continued, "I see we have the pleasure of a second visit from Mrs Forest." He watched his wife leave before turning his attention to Libby and Max, lifting one hand as though blessing the visitors. The sun lit his grey hair like a halo. Long, loose robes flowed from head to toe, and as he raised his arm, a sleeve slid back to reveal a tattoo. Libby's gaze locked on the design.

He saw the direction of her eyes. "You're interested in my tattoo?" He uncovered the length of the tattooed snake that wound around his right elbow, travelling up his arm until it disappeared at the shoulder. "The product of my time in India."

Libby, horrified and fascinated, jumped as Max's voice rang out. "So, you follow an Indian guru?"

The man pulled down his sleeve. "I fear I have no time to chat, pleasant though that would be. I must ask you to excuse Olivia and myself, unless you'd care to join our meeting."

CHAPTER SIXTEEN

Séance

"Are you crazy?" Max hissed, his mouth close to Libby's ear, as they followed Xavier through the house and up the wide staircase.

"You don't have to come. Not your thing, I suppose."

"I'm not leaving you alone with this pair. They're stark staring mad, if you ask me."

"In that case, let's see what happens."

They passed the door of the music room where Libby had listened to the Rachmaninov, and continued on to the end of the corridor. Muffled voices sounded behind the heavy oak door as Olivia Papadopoulos pushed it wide, ushering Libby and Max into the room. A handful of people sat in armchairs that had been arranged in a horseshoe. They faced a low table, covered in a pristine white cloth, a water jug and glass, a wooden bowl, and two candles.

Xavier Papadopoulos took a position behind the table, his hands lifted in greeting. "Welcome, my friends and fellow members, as we walk the Pathway to Health. Today, we have two visitors. Some of you may recognise Mrs Forest and Mr Ramshore."

Did the small collection of smiling faces belong to an audience or a congregation? Libby's heart sank as she saw Kate Stephenson lean forward and wave. "Hello, Mrs Forest – or may I call you Libby?" With a sweeping gesture of one arm, Kate addressed the room. "Libby and I have spent time together. Let's welcome her to our small band of friends." She led a burst of applause. The twitch of Max's eyebrows betrayed surprise at seeing Kate, but not, Libby decided, displeasure.

All the onlookers were new to Libby. Three older women sat close together, a little apart from a young girl with unwashed hair who gazed glumly at bitten nails. The two remaining members of the group were men, one wearing flowing robes similar to those worn by Sandy Papadopoulos, while the other was dressed in a formal shirt, tie, and business suit.

Xavier Papadopoulos held out his arm, fingers elegantly curved, and beckoned his wife. "Some of you, I believe, have need of our endeavours today. We must try to break through the bounds of this mortal realm and reach out to another dimension."

Libby and Max shared a wry smile. It seemed

Olivia was some kind of medium, purporting to put the dead in touch with the living. Libby shot a longing look at the door. Could she slip away without being noticed? This felt like a bad mistake.

It was too late. Xavier Papadopoulos lit the candles, wafted across the room, and dimmed the light while Olivia sat at the table. Max leaned very close to whisper, "I wonder what's under that table?"

The dose of common sense calmed Libby's nerves. What harm could come from a couple of aging hippies playing at séances?

Olivia stirred something in the wooden bowl, and a sweet scent permeated through the room. She muttered something Libby couldn't catch in a slow, rhythmic monotone. Her husband, his voice deep and soothing, exhorted the listeners to concentrate on their breathing. A clock ticked, insistent and regular in the quiet room, and Libby's eyes grew heavy. She took a deep breath, squeezed both fists tight, and dug her nails into her palms, blinking hard, willing herself to stay awake.

She stole a glance at Max's face. A small smile crinkled his eyes. At once, the tension in Libby's muscles seeped away. There was no need to panic while Max was there, sensible and down to earth.

Some of the other attendees leaned forwards, hands on their knees, faces alert, as if expecting something exciting to happen, but others seemed drowsy, as though in a daze. The man in a business suit had his chin tucked into his chest, and Libby could almost believe he was dozing. Maybe he'd had a liquid lunch.

The urge to giggle took her by surprise. It must be a nervous reaction. Desperate not to draw attention, she sucked in both cheeks and held her breath. She felt rather than saw Max look her way, but dare not meet his eye for fear of bursting into wild laughter.

Xavier Papadopoulos clapped his hands, shocking Libby back to reality. Under cover of the noise, she coughed and regained control. The two women who'd been leaning forward, apparently entranced, rose and stood one on either side of Olivia. One wore a red kaftan, the other an everyday black jumper and trousers.

In the flickering candlelight, Olivia's face glowed. She closed her eyes and intoned in a deep voice, "I feel someone near." She reached out to the two women, taking their hands. "One of your departed loved ones wishes to contact you." She paused. The women's eyes never left her face as she raised their hands high above her head. "His name," she intoned, "begins with F." She paused, but no one spoke. "Or S."

The woman in black shook her head, but the

red kaftan cried out, "My father's name was Stephen."

Olivia Papadopoulos dropped the other woman's hand. "My dear, your father says you're not to worry. He's happy and reunited with his long-time love, who crossed over before him."

The woman was nodding. "My stepmother died a year ago."

"That's right."

"Can you a-ask him about my real mother. She died when I was a child, before Father remarried."

Olivia gave a deep sigh. "Wait, he's talking. He says your mother is there and all is well."

"But which one is he with?" The woman was trembling, agitated. "Which one is his true love? He can't be with both."

Max whispered, "Good question."

Xavier Papadopoulos stepped forward. "My dear, things are different in the Other Dimension." His voice awarded the two words audible capital letters. "On earth, we are bound by convention. Yet even here, people live happily with more than one partner. Your father is in a state of perpetual joy, his soul entwined with everyone he's ever loved."

The woman's smile illuminated her face. Libby wanted to jump up and shout at the man. How could these people be so gullible?

Perhaps she'd made a sudden movement. Papadopoulos was suddenly watching, his face expressionless. He held Libby's gaze for a long moment. Defiant, she returned the stare as he dropped a hand on his wife's shoulder. "Do you have messages for others in the room?"

Olivia was silent for a long time, breathing heavily. At last, "Ah," she moaned in a quiet, sing-song voice. "I hear another. A husband who needs to connect. He wants to make amends." She rose from her seat and paced round the room. Every head turned to follow her progress. "He needs to contact his wife. He's been searching, longing to let her know how he feels. Is there anyone here whose name begins with B or E?"

The audience looked at each other, but no one spoke. Olivia returned to her seat. She swayed, gently. "He tells me his wife uses a shortened name. Wait. It grows clearer. The full name is…" she paused. The room lay silent, her watchers holding their breath, waiting. "The name is Elizabeth."

The words hit Libby like a punch in the stomach. She stifled a gasp. The businessman further along the horseshoe jerked awake at the sound, turning to stare. Libby's chest felt squeezed tight, as though encased in steel.

Olivia intoned, "He tells me he was a bad

husband. He did wrong. He wants to tell Elizabeth he's sorry and he is watching over her."

Libby could hardly breathe for the pain in her chest. She swallowed, tasting bile. The room closed in around her, and she could stand it no longer. One hand pressed to her mouth, she scrambled past Max and ran from the room, clattering down the stairs and out through the front door into the blessed fresh air.

***

Libby wheezed, dragging air into her lungs, her head fuzzy, while the ground seemed to sway under her feet. Someone was at her elbow. She recognised Mandy's voice. "Mrs F. Whatever's the matter?" Sturdy in a pair of heavy boots, hands on hips, face creased in a worried frown, Mandy demanded, "What are you doing here?"

It took all Libby's self-control to resist throwing both arms around her young friend. She tried a smile. "N-nothing. It's nothing to worry about." The wobbly voice sounded ridiculous, as though it belonged to someone else. Libby cleared her throat, aware she'd made an exhibition of herself. "I had a shock, that's all."

She'd let that woman's nonsense upset her, but it was all a sham. Olivia Papadopoulos had been playing a mean trick. Well, if she'd wanted to frighten Libby away from investigating the Pathway to Health, she was going to be disappointed. Nevertheless, the shock of a message supposed to be from her dead husband, sickened Libby. How did the woman know so much about her? It couldn't just be luck.

She thought back over the séance. Olivia's spiel was well practised. Her husband's hand on her shoulder had been a signal. They'd probably used the trick with dozens of other vulnerable people. Most likely, everyone in the room was hoping for a message from a lost relative or friend. Why else would they put up with the Papadopoulos pair's mumbo-jumbo?

Libby had fallen for a cheap fairground trick. Furious, she waved an angry finger at Mandy. "You're not going near those con artists and their phony séance."

Mandy giggled. "Good to see you're back to normal. Had me worried for a moment, there."

"Sorry." As Libby spoke, Max appeared, his face creased with concern. He drew her close but she caught sight of Kate close behind, stiffened and pulled away. "I'm fine. It was hot in there and I can't stand the smell of incense. That's all."

Kate looked at Libby with soulful brown eyes. "It's the emotion in the room. It can be

155

overwhelming at first, but so many people find it helpful on their journey."

Libby ignored her.

Max sounded anxious. "Well, if you're OK." He peered into Libby's face, but she was too angry to read whatever message he was trying to communicate. He gave the ghost of a shrug and turned away. "Mandy, fancy meeting you here."

"I said I'd pick Kate up after the Pathway meeting. We're having another session today and it's an excuse to drive out here in my swanky new car."

Max and Kate admired Mandy's new wheels, while Libby fought to control her feelings. Max was on the warmest of terms with Kate. He didn't seem to notice anything strange about the woman, but it was obvious she was close to the Papadopoulos couple and their Pathway cult. Was he blind?

An unpleasant thought struck Libby. She'd wondered how Olivia Papadopoulos had known about her late husband. Perhaps Max had talked about him with Kate.

Surely Max would never betray Libby like that. Or would he? She bit her lip. Perhaps she didn't know him as well as she'd imagined. When they'd first met, he'd warned her he was difficult to know. Maybe she'd taken his feelings for granted…

Mandy and Kate were about to get into the car. Libby would think about Max later. For now, she wanted to extricate Mandy from the alternative therapist's tentacles and that wasn't going to be easy. "Mandy," she began. "Don't forget we planned to work on those new flavours today."

Mandy waved a hand. "Don't give it a thought, Mrs F. I'll be there in plenty of time. And I'll tell you about Kate's wonder treatment for my phobia while we work."

Kate, one foot already in the passenger side of Mandy's car, turned to wave. Her bag slid from her shoulder and fell to the floor at Libby's feet, contents spilling onto the grass verge. With a muttered exclamation, Kate bent to scoop the pile of belongings back into the bag. She grabbed a blue coin-purse, a couple of pens, a tube of extra-strong mints, and several crumpled pieces of paper, probably receipts for petrol or meals. But it was another object, twinkling in the June sun, that caught Libby's attention. A key, just like the one near Liam's body.

A second later, the key had disappeared back into Kate's bag, leaving Libby wondering if she was mistaken. It could have been an everyday front-door key.

Max waved the two women off and ushered

Libby into the Land Rover. "I can see you've got something to say."

Libby shook her head in silence. Her eyes filled with tears and she dashed the back of her hand across her face, wishing she kept a clean tissue in her handbag like sensible people did. Her head was full of questions, but for the first time since they'd met, she wondered if she could trust Max. Her feelings were a mess. She wouldn't mention Kate. Better to stick to the Papadopoulos couple.

She took a long breath. "Those two are the biggest pair of frauds I've seen for a long time." It was a relief to let her anger have an outlet. "Do you think they're charging those people for coming to their Pathway?"

"I saw a collection plate on my way out. I presume it's there for contributions, but I didn't stop to give them anything, and neither did Kate. I'm sorry it took a while for me to follow you outside. I wanted to catch the end of that little interlude."

Intrigued despite her anger, Libby asked, "What happened after I left?"

"You mean, after that very dramatic storming out?"

Libby was not yet ready to be persuaded to smile. "They frightened me. I know it was stupid, but that monotonous, ticking clock was like water dripping on my head. I couldn't stay for another moment."

"You haven't got over the whole Trevor thing yet, have you?"

Libby tried a little laugh. "I thought I had. I'd almost forgiven Trevor for the way he treated me like a doormat, but when that woman told everyone in the room what a fool I'd been, I was ashamed."

Max took her hand and, without lifting his eyes from the road, touched it to his lips. Despite the turmoil in her head, she didn't bother to pull away. Max sounded angrier than she'd ever heard him. "Trevor, far from floating happily in whatever other dimension the Papadopoulos couple describe, deserves to suffer for what he did."

Libby took a moment. "No, I wouldn't wish that on anyone, not even Trevor. I don't know what happens after death, but maybe there's a reckoning. Who knows? Anyway, my husband's gone and I'm not going to let him back into my life."

"Good for you." Max let go of her hand to change gear. They drove for a while in something that passed for companionable silence.

"By the way," Max sounded business-like. "I

took a call from Joe as I was leaving the séance. He wants to talk to us and it sounds important."

***

Constable Evans met Max and Libby at the police station. She knew him well. A big, florid man, overweight and sadly lacking in social graces, he'd probably remain a constable his entire career. He shook Max's hand, and grunted at Libby. She sighed. Max always seemed to be accepted as one of the boys, while most of the police seemed determined to resent her.

The interview room, where they were to meet Joe, was a plain cube. It held a coffee table, with a small two-seater settee arranged next to it, opposite a couple of armchairs. Two hard wooden chairs leaned against the walls and a camera was fixed high on the wall. Joe nodded towards the lens. "We won't need to record our interview. You're not a suspect, this time." Libby opened her mouth, saw the twinkle in Joe's eye and let her jaw snap shut as she realised he was teasing.

A police constable arrived with three coffee cups, all with the battered look of office mugs more used to a quick rinse under the tap than a thorough cycle in the dishwasher. Libby struggled with a small carton of long-life milk. As ever, a few drops scattered across her shirt. She'd never learned the knack of opening those things. She took a careful sip from the mug, tried not to wince, and placed it back on the table.

"Sorry about the coffee." Joe grinned. "Not up to your standards, I'm afraid, but I wanted to show you this as soon as possible." From a cardboard carton, he drew out a couple of plastic zip-lock bags and placed them on the table. "This is evidence, so I can't take it out of the bag, but I wondered what you made of it."

Max said, "That's the key you found near Liam's body, I suppose?"

Joe nodded. "It is, but what I really wanted to show you was this." He pointed to the other bag. "We found a box in Liam's bedsit that the key fitted. These were inside."

Libby and Max leaned forward to look at the slips of paper inside the bag. There were half a dozen lines of printed letters and numbers on the paper. Libby squinted. "Those aren't real words."

"Afraid not. I wondered if they meant anything to you."

Libby shrugged.

Joe said, "Do you remember that business of the body at the lighthouse?"

She smiled. "Of course I do. It was the first time we'd met and you thought I was an interfering old woman."

Joe side-stepped that. "You solved that crime by working out a code."

Libby guessed what was coming. "That was a bit of a fluke, to be honest. It's not as though I'm a crossword puzzler."

Max was frowning at the letters. "These look like passwords, to me."

Joe said, "That's what we thought. Funny thing is, Liam doesn't seem to have a computer. Just his phone. We tried to find something the passwords fitted, but so far, we've hit a wall. Maybe they're not passwords at all, but some kind of code. Any chance of you helping crack it?"

Max pointed at the cardboard box. "Is there anything else to point us in the right direction?"

Joe pulled out one more bag. "Just these candles. As you can see, they're already half burned."

Libby leaned forward until her nose was almost on the plastic bag. "I can smell something, but it's faint, through the plastic. Max, can you smell it? Is it incense?"

Joe nodded. "That's what we thought. Now, why would a young chap like Liam burn incense candles? We wondered if he used them with girlfriends. You know, to set the tone for a romantic evening, but if that's the case, why hide them away?"

Max told him about the Papadopoulos couple, the séance they'd attended, and the smell of incense in the room. Joe beamed. "Great stuff. Could be a link between this Pathway affair and Liam. Can I get you another cup of coffee to celebrate?"

"Not likely," Libby answered without thinking. "Are there any fingerprints or anything-er-forensic?"

"Well, apart from Liam's fingerprints and bits of fibres that match bedding and so on from his bedsit, there's half a thumbprint on one of the candles that we haven't been able to match. With a bit of luck we'll find it belongs to one of your Papadopoulos friends."

CHAPTER SEVENTEEN

Lunch

Glad to be back at the bakery next day, far away from séances, missing women, and dead farmhands, Libby slid a small loaf into a strong paper bag, for the flower shop lady. "Anything else I can get for you? Your usual cream meringues?"

The woman shook her head. "Can't stop. Too much to do." She hurried to the door, almost colliding with Max, and scampered down the street, heading to the right, away from her own shop.

Max grinned and spoke to Libby, "Can I whisk you away for lunch, later?"

They'd hardly spoken since returning from the police station. Libby, still on edge and longing for a quiet evening, had pleaded a headache and the need to talk to Robert, and returned home alone. She'd hoped a good night's sleep would improve her mood, but Robert and she had talked far into the night. He'd heard nothing from Sarah. He'd been calling and texting her all day, but either she'd switched off her mobile phone or it had run out of battery. "I can't decide which is worse – is she running away from me, or has something terrible happened?" He'd lifted Fuzzy and buried his face in the cat's fur. "You were right about the police. They say there's no reason to worry, yet."

Joe had said the same thing to Libby. A missing adult driving away in their own car, even a newly-wed, wouldn't trigger a major police search for several days.

Robert had continued, "I've spoken to everyone I can think of. All her friends and work colleagues. Nobody knows what's going on."

Libby, sick at heart, had struggled to think of something to comfort him. "Look, Belinda's gone as well. They must be together. That's good, isn't it? I'm sure they won't come to any harm." She hoped she was right. She hated to see Robert in such a state of despair. In just a day, he'd gone from a besotted new husband to a nail-biting wreck. If only she could mother him with ice cream, as she had in the old days when he fell off his bike. "If she's not back in a couple of days, I'm sure the police will start searching in earnest."

After persuading Robert to get some sleep, and falling into her own bed in the small hours, Libby had woken tired and despondent. Robert had still been asleep when she'd left the house.

Now, Libby frowned at Max. She stammered, "I-I suppose so." She checked no one was around to hear. "What did you want to talk about? I had a thought about Liam's notes—" She broke off as two schoolboys crashed through the door, fighting to be first to the counter, jostling each other and howling with laughter.

Max leaned against the glass showcase, admiring Libby's chocolates. "What if I just want the pleasure of your company?"

Libby served the boys with blueberry muffins, their sniggers fading under Max's icy stare. "We'll have to eat fast. I promised to do the afternoon shift and Frank's in a spin about this new patisserie. He's worried about business, and judging by that woman's shifty behaviour, I've a feeling he may be right. Could we go somewhere close?"

"Midday, then. At the Lighthouse?"

Once at the pub, they settled at a table in the corner and studied the menu. "Sometimes, pub food is just what I need," Max said. "Not that it's ever as good as yours, of course."

Libby took a breath, ready to bring up the subject of Kate Stephenson. She changed her mind. She didn't want to quarrel in public. "Why did you want to meet?"

Max didn't answer. Instead, he glanced round the room, nodding to a couple of acquaintances at another table. Libby realised he'd deliberately picked a table at a fair distance from anyone else. His expression was grim.

Libby replaced the menu on the table. "Come on, out with it." He'd never seemed reluctant to talk before. This must be bad news.

"I've found out a little more about your son's new in-laws. I took a look at the farm's accounts."

"I take it you don't mean the public ones filed at Companies House?"

He gave his lopsided smile. "Don't ask too many questions about how I found them, but I discovered the official accounts bear little resemblance to another set, hidden behind a complicated series of screens and passwords."

"Quite the hacker, aren't you?"

"I learned a thing or two from my geeky colleagues in the past. Do you want to know what I discovered, or will you give me up to the authorities?"

"We'll see. Tell me."

A waitress approached. Libby and Max each ordered a ploughman's lunch, and Max waited until she'd retreated to the kitchen before continuing. "That farm's doing a great deal better than you'd imagine, given the recent problems with the price of milk and so on."

"Maybe they've been diversifying. They make cheese and yoghurt."

He nodded. "I found all that. They're managing better than most, but not well enough to cover large payments coming in and going out. Nothing illegal, but very lucrative. There are sums of money received from dozens of people, all over the world, described as 'services'."

"Really? What sort of services. Not..." An image of Belinda dressed as an old-school madam and running a massage parlour sprang into Libby's head.

Max laughed. "Not those services. I dug a little further and discovered they use a website that sends out automated email sequences."

"There's nothing wrong with those. I use one to contact customers, to check their orders have arrived and tell them about new lines and so on. I write the emails, and the service sends them out at intervals."

She sat back as the waitress delivered plates piled high with ham, crusty bread, salad and chutney. "To be honest, I don't do any of that. Mandy's been in charge of it all, updating the business. She understands how it works. She says every business has an on-line presence nowadays, and she's right. Sales have rocketed. Why shouldn't

Belinda and Mike do the same?"

Max was nodding. "Exactly. The problem is, the emails don't go out under the farm's name."

Libby stopped, a forkful of local-cured ham on the way to her mouth. "What name are they using? No. Wait. Don't tell me. The Pathway to Health?" Max nodded. Libby replaced the fork on her plate, leaving her food half eaten. "The Papadopoulos cult."

"Exactly. It seems Mike and Belinda's farm is running a separate, very lucrative business with Olivia and Xavier."

Libby looked at her watch and swore. "There's no time to talk more. I've got to get back."

Max said, "Come round for supper. Joe and Claire are coming. Joe wants to know what I've found, even though it doesn't appear to relate to Liam's death." He grabbed her hand. "Maybe we'll find time to talk, soon."

CHAPTER EIGHTEEN

Supper

To Libby's surprise, Mandy opened Max's door that evening, beaming. "We think you need cheering up." Libby's throat contracted. She felt wretched. Beside herself with worry about Robert and deeply upset by the séance, she'd pushed her worries about Max and Kate deep down inside, but she couldn't forget.

Robert was still at her cottage, unable to bear the thought of living alone in rented accommodation while he should have been on honeymoon, touring the West Country. She'd been tempted to bring him along, but he wanted to spend the evening phoning Sarah's friends again. He'd waved Libby off with Fuzzy cradled in his arms, insisting he would be fine, but he looked ten years older and thoroughly miserable.

Max's friend Reginald, bigger and more positive than ever, was leaving for the States in a few weeks. Libby cast a quick glance at Mandy, wondering how she'd deal with the loss.

Claire had brought food, refusing to let Libby near the cooker. "You cook all the time. If you don't mind eating simple food…"

Joe snorted, on his way to the fridge for ice. "She means, if you don't mind your chicken burned to a crisp."

He ducked as Claire threw a tea towel. "Of course, he's right," she admitted. "I can't cook for toffee."

Mandy made a noise between a cough and a snort. "I'm sorry," she spluttered. "What does that even mean?"

Max patted her on the head with mock condescension. "You young things…"

Joe spent half an hour in the kitchen, mixing cocktails. Reginald accepted a Martini and boomed, "Is this something they teach at your British Police College, Joe? Vodka martini, shaken, not stirred, a la James Bond?"

Max stuck with beer. "I need a clear head. There are so many bits and pieces of information to draw together."

"Personally, I think better after a Margarita," Libby insisted. "Or at least, I think I think better. Which probably isn't the same thing at all."

Mandy leaned over and grabbed her glass. "How many have you had, Mrs F? You do know that's almost pure spirits, don't you?"

Libby waved a hand in the air. "Don't mind me. Max is going to tell us what he found out about Handiwater Farm."

Max flipped up the lid of his laptop. "I'll show you." They gathered at his shoulder and he turned the screen so they could all see.

First, he brought up a picture of the farm. "This is the official website. As you see, it has tabs leading to pages of information about the farm itself, products for sale, a few moody shots of the cattle coming in for milking at dawn, that sort of thing."

Joe leaned over and clicked through a couple of tabs. "Nothing odd there, so far as I can see."

"That's right. However, if we go to this page of links…" Max scrolled down a long page. "Here it is. A link to the Pathway. If we follow it, this is what we find."

The screen changed, opening up a different site. Libby peered at the screen. "It's a typical New Age sort of page. The kind you'd expect from alternative healers, full of rainbows and unicorns." She fell silent, thinking of Kate Stephenson.

"That's right. All above board, with offers of astrology readings, interactive fortune telling, and lucky numbers. Silly stuff, but it seems harmless. However, I approached it from a different angle, using what they call the Dark Web."

Claire's eyes were on stalks. "Isn't that the place where people buy drugs and weapons? Things not supposed to be for sale?"

Max shrugged. "There's some stuff on there you really don't want to see. It's a set of web pages hidden from the normal user, where you have to use a special browser to get in. Hackers use it all the time. I dug around and came across some interesting information about the Pathway's activities. For one thing, they have deep, hidden links to the Silk Road, an on-line source of illegal substances. You can't use banks or even PayPal there. They deal in bitcoins, the on-line currency."

Mandy shivered, theatrically. "How very sinister."

Reginald's bear hug almost pulled her off her feet. "Don't worry about it."

Joe was leaning forward, to get a better view. "Some of my colleagues have to be experts on these areas of the web. It's a constant battle to keep up with all the frauds, phishers, and scammers around."

His father nodded. "I'm not surprised. Now, the Pathway appears to have access to sites with information that should be private. For example, databases of names and personal information that are supposed to be secure and encrypted."

Claire sounded thoughtful. "I've heard of

hackers getting hold of credit card information and pretending to be other people."

"That's right." Joe was nodding. "Identity theft. It happens often, these days. Is that what the Pathway's up to?"

Max stretched, rubbing the back of his neck. "Not quite. They've been collecting other kinds of information. Personal stuff to use against people."

As he spoke, Libby's brain clicked into gear. She winced. "Is that how Olivia knew about my husband, and how she could target me at the séance? She's seen information about me. She knows all about Trevor..." She groaned. The Papadopoulos couple knew her innermost secrets. She remembered Xavier's supercilious smile when she met him at the wedding and the way he'd lingered on her name. The thought brought acid bile into her mouth.

She swallowed. "How else are they using the information they steal, apart from fake séances?"

"Someone's been running a series of scams."

"Who? Not Mike or Belinda? Surely, they wouldn't get involved—" She bit off the words. Belinda had disappeared. Did she know about the Papadopoulos couple's scams? If so, she could be in danger, and Sarah with her.

As she pondered, Libby started to collect plates. Mandy jumped up. "You leave it to us, Mrs

F." Claire and Reginald followed Mandy into the kitchen.

"About that list I showed you," Joe began, seizing the moment alone with Libby and Max. "I can't talk about police business with everyone here, but I wanted to tell you we had another look in Liam's place, but there's definitely no sign of a computer. We still have no idea what the passwords unlock."

Libby murmured, "What if…"

The two men fell silent, watching, but she shook her head. The myriad ideas in her head didn't quite make sense. "No. I had a thought, but it's gone. I'm getting muddled. Cults and scams and people disappearing. Not to mention Liam's death and his secret passwords. I wonder what we're missing in all this."

Joe said, "There's one thing. It doesn't take us any further, but I thought you'd want to know about the ring."

Max made a face. "What ring?"

"That fight at the wedding, remember? Over the missing ring?"

"The one Liam stole?"

Libby interrupted. "Or at least Tim said he stole it."

"Well, it's a fake. Professionally set, but pure glass. Worth almost nothing. So what the old lady was making such a fuss about, I can't imagine."

Max raised an eyebrow. "Another piece of the jigsaw that makes little sense." He scratched his head with one arm of his reading glasses, leaving his hair in spikes, and yawned. "It's hard to see the wood for the trees, sometimes. Let's let our minds work on it while we're asleep. Libby and I will talk it through tomorrow morning. If we come up with anything, we'll phone you, Joe."

Mandy returned, just as he finished speaking. "Don't forget we're working on those new chocolate flavours tomorrow, Mrs F. Raspberry and ginger. Yummy."

Libby picked up her bag. "I'll start Mandy off tomorrow morning and come back here."

He shrugged. "Bear and I will be waiting."

CHAPTER NINETEEN

Handiwater

Mandy arrived bright and early next morning. Libby held a finger to her lips and whispered, "Come into the kitchen. Robert's still asleep."

Mandy giggled. "Won't he have a shock when he finds me here?"

"I'm sure you'll cheer him up."

She left Mandy mixing ingredients, and headed for the car. For once, she felt in no hurry to see Max. She couldn't get Kate Stephenson out of her head.

She let in the clutch, thinking of Kate's annoyingly pretty face. Alternative therapy, indeed. Oh well. She might as well admit it. She was jealous. And with good reason. Even Mandy seemed to think the sun shone out of Kate Stephenson's—

Libby's foot hit the brake as a thought flashed into her head.

The Fiat behind squealed to a halt, inches from the Citroen's rear end. Libby pretended not to see the driver's rude gesture and sat for a long while, thinking. What was it Mike had said? He hated computers. Someone, though, must be using one for farm business. It would be almost impossible for a working farm to exist without computers, and she knew they had a website. Someone must work on it.

Belinda's machine had been full of personal emails and shopping sites, with nothing about the farm. So, where was the farm's computer, and who used it? If it wasn't Mike, and his son Tim refused to have anything to do with the farm, there was only one other person: Liam Weston.

With a buzz of excitement, Libby remembered. Mike had said he relied on Liam to print out anything he needed to see. She was right, Liam was the farm's computing expert.

She grinned, pleased to be a step ahead of Max. He could go on hacking into the farm's files, but why should Libby let him have all the fun? If Liam kept farm records, chances were he was the one working with Xavier Papadopoulos. Libby didn't know what they were up to, but it was certainly secret and probably illegal.

Liam had no computer at his own home, so all his information must be at the farm. What better place to hide things than on files no one else ever used, hidden in plain sight on someone else's property? Those files would tell Libby what was going on out there in the villages of Exmoor. She was certain of it. She laughed aloud. She would discover the truth and steal a march on Max. That would teach him to make eyes at Kate Stephenson.

***

The Citroen squealed to a halt at Handiwater Farm. Libby ran to the house and hammered on the door, but no one came. Shipley, excited by the activity, leaped at the door. Libby pulled him away and moved to the window. Shielding her eyes from the sun's reflection, she squinted until she saw Mike, slumped at the kitchen table, staring into space. Libby banged on the door and shouted. He turned his head, his red-rimmed eyes betraying despair. Slowly, he rose and let Libby and Shipley into the house. She bit back a comment on his appearance. "Did you sleep last night?"

He shook his head. "I can't manage so much as a catnap without Belinda. She's never stayed away so long before." He drew a shuddering breath. "Don't know what I'll do if she doesn't come home. And Sarah as well. Both my women."

The house was silent, except for the ticking of the kitchen clock. "Where's Tim?"

"I sent him away. Fussing around, he was,

blaming Liam for everything. They never got on, those two."

Libby longed to ask if he'd said anything like that to the police. Did Tim's own father think he had something to do with the farm hand's death? She'd ask him later. Liam was beyond help, but the longer Belinda and Sarah were missing, the more likely it seemed they were in danger. Upsetting Mike further would just delay matters.

She took a long look at the farmer's gaunt face. Before she could get any sense out of him, he needed help. She doubted he'd eaten a square meal since his wife left. "I don't suppose you've had breakfast?"

Gathering all her patience, Libby cooked eggs and bacon, and waited until Mike had pushed bacon round his plate and torn minute pieces from a slice of bread before asking to see the computer.

"In the office. Other end of the house." The farmer showed no interest in why Libby wanted to use it. The man's lethargy began to grate on Libby's nerves. Why wasn't he trying to find his wife and daughter, instead of sitting in a puddle of gloom? She couldn't imagine Max sitting at home, doing nothing, if she'd gone missing. Not even if his affections had shifted—she clicked her tongue, annoyed at herself. Worrying about Max was a distraction she didn't need just now.

"Come with me, Shipley." She hurried down the corridor to the farm office, in search of the business's computer. There it was, in plain sight on the desk in the middle of the office. Libby hadn't spared it a glance before, when she'd been concentrating on Belinda's desk.

Libby pulled out her notebook, turned to the page of passwords, and switched on the machine.

The computer accepted the second password on Liam's list and a screen full of icons opened. Libby grinned. It felt good to be right, sometimes. The glow of success only lasted a moment or two, though. Where should she go next?

She found the farm website that Max had shown them last night, but clicked away. She'd leave Max to go down that route. She was looking for something more personal to Liam Weston.

For half an hour she clicked through random files, finding nothing beyond innocuous Word files of business letters and Excel spreadsheets, full of animal numbers, milk quotas, and details of subsidy payments. These were the tools Mandy had been struggling to persuade her to use for her business.

Nothing jarred or seemed out of place, and there were only a couple of files left unopened. Libby's neck ached and her eyes itched from staring at the screen. She yawned and clicked on one of the remaining files.

It demanded another password. Libby sat straighter and ran a finger down Liam's password list. After a couple of false starts, just as she feared another mistake would lock her out of the file for ever, the file opened.

At first glance, there was little to warrant such secrecy. The file was a simple list of names. Some were familiar: Belinda, Sarah, Olivia and Xavier Papadopoulos, Kate Stephenson. Libby murmured, "The Pathway?" Several last names recurred often. That was common in this part of the world, where families had lived, worked the land, and intermarried for generations. Watson, Meres, Appleby, Hambledon: Libby had met dozens of people sharing those names. She visualised them, trying to imagine each as a member of the cult.

Appleby. She knew an Appleby, but she couldn't place them. She tilted her chair back, rubbing her nose, trying to visualise where she had been when she heard the name. Her mouth fell open. Lady Antonia Appleby was Belinda's aged aunt. Libby could remember her now: Lady Antonia, full of old-fashioned airs and graces but forgetful and vague, making a fuss at the wedding about a worthless ring. The old lady must have known it had no value.

Or did she? The woman had been distraught. She was old, and hardly lucid at times. A twinge of guilt hit Libby. She'd dismissed the woman's panic over the loss of a valueless piece of costume jewellery, putting it down to age and some kind of mild dementia. Instead, she'd focused on the animosity between Liam and Tim and never stopped to wonder about the ring's value. She'd find out about that ring later.

She pasted the list of names into an email and sent it to her own inbox. She was focused on the last remaining file, hoping it would contain even more information.

Sure enough, she needed the last of Liam's passwords to open the spreadsheet. She held her breath as it opened to show three columns of information. The first was a series of dates, beginning a year ago, and ending in May. The second column was a list of places. She recognised some of them: Dulverton, Williton, and Watchet were all Somerset towns.

Puzzled, she turned to the third column, which contained hyperlinks. She clicked on one and gasped as a photograph opened up. There was Kate Stephenson, her arms round someone with his back to the camera, eyes closed, mouth half-open in the prelude to a kiss. For a second, Libby's stomach seemed to turn over. Then she relaxed.

The man wasn't Max.

She peered more closely, her heart rate returning to normal, but she couldn't identify the man in the photo.

She tried another link from the file, and found another image. Taken from the outside, looking in through a window, it showed Kate Stephenson and the same man. This time, both were naked. Libby smiled as she recognised the curtains in Abbott House, Kate's home.

She pulled a mint from an old packet in her bag and sucked, as a series of events clicked into place in her mind like dots joining up to make an outline; Kate, Belinda's links to the Pathway, her disappearance, and the strange affair of the worthless ring.

Libby swallowed the last of the mint and shut down the computer. She knew where she had to go.

Her phone rang. "Yes?"

Max said, "Where are you? I thought you were coming round this morning. Bear's furious, and I'm…" He hesitated. "I'm missing you."

A warm glow flooded Libby's veins, but there was no time to talk. She gabbled, "I've cracked it. I've been looking at the farm computer and I know what this is all about. Give me Lady Antonia's address and meet me there. Hurry up,

I'm on my way."

"Hold on," Max shouted. "Wait for me. Don't do anything until I get there."

Libby dropped the phone in her bag before he could protest, and hurried to the kitchen.

Mike sat where she'd left him, his face vacant. She hesitated. He was in no fit state to answer questions. Anyway, she had no need to ask. She dropped a hand on his shoulder. "You should have told us, Mike."

"What?"

"Never mind. Stay here, I'll be back soon." Libby grabbed Shipley and left at a run, leaving behind Mike's plaintive voice, begging her to explain what on earth was going on.

CHAPTER TWENTY

The house

Gravel screeched under the car's wheels as Libby accelerated away, speeding down the twisting lanes until she turned onto the main road and hit the back of a queue of traffic travelling at less than ten miles an hour.

Thumping the steering wheel, she leaned sideways, trying to see the blockage. A tractor lumbered ahead, filling the road, leaving no room to pass. Frustrated, taut muscles screaming, Libby changed down until she was crawling in second gear.

Just as she was about to scream with frustration, the tractor found a lay-by and let the queue of traffic pass.

At last, she reached Lady Antonia's home. Libby steered between two pillars topped with stone pineapples, drove past a tiny church along a narrow avenue, hedged on either side by beeches, and arrived at an impressive Georgian manor house. Libby counted eight rows of windows, dark and uninviting despite the early afternoon sun. Libby's skin crawled. Under other circumstances, she'd think the house charming and old-fashioned, but her heart was pumping with fear for Sarah and Belinda.

She ran up the short flight of carved stone steps to hammer on the door. There was no reply, so she ran round the house to the back garden, where a spacious lawn led down to an ornamental lake. Lilies floated serenely on the surface.

There was no one in sight.

Shipley sniffed round the garden, found a scent, and nose close to the floor, ran down the path and back. "What is it, Shipley? Can you smell something strange?"

The dog stopped, nose in the air, four legs rigid. Libby knelt beside him. "What is it?" She followed his gaze. "Are you pointing at something?"

Directly in the line of the dog's sight was a set of outhouses, probably built as stabling for horses, but no equine heads poked over the half doors today. With an anxious glance back at the house, Libby walked towards the nearest stable, her pulse racing. She had one hand on the wood, ready to push it open, when Shipley barked, once. "Not that one?"

She moved to the next door, Shipley at her

heels. "Is this the way?"

The door opened easily. The outhouse was full of junk. She saw old chairs and an ancient mangle, a relic from the days of washing clothes by hand. A musty smell emanated from a pile of rolled carpet. Wrinkling her nose, Libby muttered to the dog, "Is that what you can smell? Old rugs?"

The dog ignored her. Tail in the air, nose to the ground, he pushed past heaps of rubbish to the other end of the building, where he stopped at the wall, body rigid.

At first, Libby could see nothing unusual. Just wooden slats. She looked more closely. One area of wood was cleaner than the rest. She ran tentative fingers across the surface. The wood moved under her hand. She pushed, hard, and it swung open so fast she almost overbalanced.

She steadied herself, grasping at the door frame. The ground below her feet pitched sharply down as steps led away into the blackness. Remembering one of the tricks Mandy had shown her, she switched on her phone to light the way, and set off down the stairs. "Come on, Shipley," she whispered. "I'm not going down there alone."

***

Blood thundering in her ears, Libby descended

the steps, one hand touching the wall, the other holding the phone. Shipley, close behind, growled quietly.

The steps turned sharp left and Libby followed, her hand trembling, the light flickering over the walls. What was that? She stopped and Shipley scrambled past, almost knocking her over, and galloped across the floor. Libby shone her phone light round the space, but could see nothing except racks of wine bottles lining the walls. The air in the cellar was cool and dry.

"There's nothing here, Shipley. It's just a wine cellar." Weak with relief, Libby examined the bottles more closely. Some were covered in dust, while others looked more recent, but there was nothing unusual about any of them. Shipley snuffled in the corner. "What have you found?"

Aiming her light with care, she could make out cracks where the walls met the wooden floor. "Rats." Libby shuddered. "That's what you were chasing. And I thought you were leading me to something important."

A voice boomed from the top of the steps. "I hope you haven't disturbed my bottles."

Libby spun round. "Lady Antonia," she gulped, filled with sudden guilt. "Er, no. I was just-er-just… I'll come back up."

"Will you?"

Libby tensed, suddenly motionless as she recognised the man's voice.

John Canterbury, the friendly rector, had joined the old woman.

Libby rested her foot on the first step, shining her light upwards. The rector's eyes glittered. "Time to stop snooping about, I think. Antonia, get back inside the house. Make coffee or something."

"What do you—" Libby stopped. "Where are Belinda and Sarah?"

The rector descended the stairs, slowly, his face menacing in the single beam of light. "Not here, I'm afraid. And you won't be seeing them. We're all very tired of you poking your nose into our business. It's time to stop."

Libby licked dry lips, searching for something to use as a weapon.

"I'm sorry, my dear," the rector went on. "We can't tolerate any more of your interference—" He stopped speaking as a deafening torrent of barking echoed round the cellar.

Lurching forward, the rector made a grab for the doorway, but his feet slipped on the narrow steps. For a long moment, he teetered at the top of the stairs, trying to regain his balance, before his feet slipped on the narrow steps and he fell.

Libby clutched at his jacket as he fell past her,

but the weight of his body pulled it from her grasp, and with a sickening crack, his head hit the floor. Bear, still barking, appeared in the gloom at Libby's side.

Max followed, running down the steps. "Bear, that's enough." His hand brushed Libby's shoulder. "Are you OK?"

As she nodded, he crouched by the rector's side and felt for a pulse in his neck. "He's still alive." Max pulled out his phone and swore. "No reception down here."

CHAPTER TWENTY ONE

Candles

Libby blinked against the daylight streaming down the cellar steps. She gasped as she saw Belinda, face dirty, usually tidy hair in greasy spikes, scrubbing away tears with a grubby handkerchief. Libby laughed aloud. Sarah was there, too, outside the stable, her phone to her ear, laughing and crying at the same time. "Robert? It's all over. I'm safe."

"Where's Antonia?"

Belinda's eyes were red. "She's lying down. She's even more confused than usual, now. "

"But, what are you all doing here? I mean, I thought we'd find you here, but Shipley took me to the cellar and then…" Libby felt a sob rise in her throat, now the drama was over. She bit her lip, determined not to cry.

Max took her hand. "Shipley needs a little more training if he's going to be useful as a sniffer dog. I imagine he was taking you to the rats. But he wasn't far away from Sarah and Belinda, locked in the next stable. The rector drugged them both to keep them quiet."

Libby made a face. "The rector had me fooled. He seemed so…"

"Quite. He put on a good show, and took us both in, but he's a wicked man. By the way, I'm impressed with your improved IT skills, if they led you straight here."

Libby managed a smile. "It's Mandy's doing. She gives me lessons. Liam kept all the information I needed on the farm computer. But, go on. Did the rector kidnap Belinda? And Sarah as well? Why would he do such a thing?"

Max looked at Belinda. She twisted her hands together, as if washing them clean. Her eyes were over-bright. "My aunt has a vast inheritance stashed away. She's been suffering from dementia for a long time, and the rector started visiting, helping her. At least, we thought that was what he was doing. I suppose he wanted to get his hands on her fortune."

Belinda's face was scarlet. "I knew the money would come to us, eventually. I came to ask my aunt for a loan one day, and the rector was here. He must have overheard my aunt refuse to give me any money while she was alive. I was getting desperate. I had to pay, you see, to get rid of…" She put her head in her hands, whispering, "To get rid of the curse."

Libby shook her head. "Pay? Who were you paying? The rector?"

Belinda shook her head. "No, not John. The Pathway. The Pathway, and Kate Stephenson."

Libby groaned. "You were hooked by those séances? We went to one. It's all a load of old hokum. The Papadopoulos couple prey on vulnerable people who've lost a partner, or a parent. They find out things about you, and fool you into thinking they're in touch with the dead."

Belinda shot a glance at Libby, through misty eyes. "You too?"

Libby chuckled. "I could have been taken in, perhaps, but they didn't realise the last person I wanted to hear from was my dead husband. All the same, I can see why you believed them, and they gave me a bad shock."

Belinda's smile was watery. "Olivia said my mother had an important message for me. She said I was in danger, but I could be helped. Kate Stephenson was there that day. She told me she could see an aura round my head, and that someone had put a-a curse on me." She began to sob. "I'm sorry, it sounds so silly."

Sarah put her arms round her mother. "Don't worry. It's all over."

Belinda took a deep breath. "Kate said she

could help lift the curse, and she'd do it for nothing because we were friends. All I had to do was pay for some special candles."

"I gave her a few pounds – hardly anything – for the candles. Then she made an appointment and I went to her house. She sat at her little table for a while, telling me about my aura, and how someone must have put the curse on me when I was young. When I was about thirteen, she said."

Libby winced. "Everyone has arguments with other children at that age. Especially girls. And they can be cruel."

"There were a few kids at school who used to bully me. They said I was posh. They used to steal from my school bag, scribble on my homework, that kind of thing. It sounds stupid, now, but it really hurt and I was scared of them. Especially one girl, who was big for her age. She used to come right up to me and spit."

Belinda's face screwed up in pain as she remembered. "When Kate told me about the curse, I remembered those girls, and I thought they might have really hexed me. Then, Kate showed me an egg. Just an ordinary egg. She said it was from the chicken in the nearby farm, but it would show if I had truly been cursed."

Belinda's face was scarlet. "I can't believe I fell for it."

Max said, "You wouldn't be the first to fall for a psychic scam. There are plenty on the internet."

With a grateful smile, Belinda went on, "She touched that stupid egg to my head and made me breathe on it, and then she smashed it on a plate. It was horrible. Mostly, it was normal egg white and yolk, all mixed up, but there were also a few black things, like apple pips, in with the yolk."

Max's voice held an undertone of cold fury. "You didn't go back there, did you?"

Belinda nodded. "Kate said there was a definite curse on me, and she could lift it, but—"

Libby interrupted. "Let me guess. It would be expensive?"

"She had to buy special crystals. She said it usually cost thousands of pounds, but she'd let me pay a little each month to the Pathway, because she wanted to help."

Max said, "You handed over the money, but the so-called curse was too strong to be dealt with in one session, so they needed more…"

Belinda nodded, sobbing too hard to talk.

Libby remembered the email to Lady Antonia she'd read in Belinda's inbox, talking about borrowing jewellery. "In the end, you owed thousands of pounds and you ran out of money. You couldn't get out of her clutches, so you borrowed some of your aunt's jewellery, pretending it was for Sarah's wedding, sold the ring and had it replaced by a fake."

Belinda blew her nose. "I was so scared. I'd stopped going to the Pathway meetings, but Olivia kept ringing up and sending me emails. They were threats, really, though not in so many words. I'd plucked up enough courage to ask you for help, but when Xavier saw us talking at the wedding, I didn't dare."

"Did you tell anyone about your money worries?"

Belinda bit her lip. "I told the rector. Mr Canterbury."

***

An ambulance siren sounded in the distance. As if on cue, the rector groaned and opened his eyes. He tried to struggle to his feet. Max smiled, his eyes steely. "Don't bother. The police are on their way. I'm rather hoping you've broken a bone or two."

"That dog of yours tried to kill me."

Bear growled, but Max held him tight. "Don't bother. We know what you've been up to, with your friends in the Pathway cult. Psychic scams, that's what they call the business you're all in: you, Xavier and Olivia Papadopoulos."

"And your lover, Kate." Libby's intervention caused a sensation. She grinned at Max's startled face, before turning back to the rector. "Don't try to deny it. Liam kept photos of you both. You've been having an affair, and he found out. That's why you killed Liam Weston."

Max's mouth dropped open. Libby didn't meet his eye. "Blackmail," she went on. "Liam was blackmailing you about your affair. He's been pulling everyone's strings. He had a hold on all of you, one way and another. He was behind the Pathway, using Xavier's charisma, his clothes, and Olivia's talent for pretending to be a medium. They've been working with Liam. He set up the business and ran it from Handiwater Farm. At the same time, he learned your secrets and blackmailed you all."

The rector scanned the circle of angry faces, desperation in his eyes. "Those photos would have finished me. Imagine a man in my position, caught having an affair. My wife would never forgive me." The self-pitying whine made Libby shiver. "I paid that monster to keep him quiet, but he was never satisfied. He wanted more and more money, bleeding me dry, until I couldn't stand it any longer. Liam Weston was evil—pure evil."

A cunning smile curled his lips. "He knew everyone's secrets." He glared directly at Belinda, a hint of hysteria in his voice as he sneered, "You let him into your lives. More fool you."

Tired of his self-justification, Libby stayed practical. "What did you use to drug him, so he'd crash the tractor?"

"Rohypnol." The rector giggled, the sound shocking. "The date-rape drug. It's easy to get hold of it these days, if you know how—"

"Your wife," Libby interrupted, remembering their conversation at the rector's house. "She's a pharmacist."

"Always so pleased to share her specialist knowledge." The venom in his voice suggested little love lost between the rector and his wife. "Thinks she's a cut above me. Like so many of you."

Max steered him back. "The Rohypnol. How did you get Liam to take it?"

"Easiest thing in the world. I'm the rector. Everyone opens their doors to me. Even though he was blackmailing me, it never occurred to Liam Weston I'd try to harm him, the idiot. Not as clever as he thought, was he?"

He giggled again. "I had a cup of coffee with Liam before he went off on his tractor. I'd tried it several times. It didn't work at first, but he didn't suspect anything. He just thought he'd had too much to drink." His smile was cruel. "It worked in the end."

Libby and Max exchanged glances. "The poison that leaves no trace."

Max's mouth was set. "Not from the Amazon rainforest, but more effective."

For a moment, she was silent, thinking hard. Finally, she admitted, "We were wrong about Tim, thinking he was jealous of Liam. What if it was the other way round?" She turned to Belinda. "I think Liam hated you for surviving the foot and mouth, while his own father was ruined and committed suicide. Liam was left with nothing, while you had everything. You trusted him, giving him access to the farm, the computer, and the house."

How dreadful to discover someone knows all your innermost secrets. "I bet he loved reading your emails. He knew you'd borrowed your aunt's jewellery. It wouldn't take him long to put two and two together and realise the ring was a fake. He really did steal it at the wedding, and made sure Tim saw him pick it up, so there'd be a fight. He wanted to draw attention to the ring so he could blackmail you, Belinda."

The rector said, "The world's better off without that boy. Born wicked, he was. I've done the world a favour."

The rictus grin he flashed at Belinda sent a chill up Libby's spine as she went on, thinking aloud. "Liam's probably been stealing from you for years, building up funds for his new herd. With that, the proceeds from blackmail, and the Pathway's psychic scams, he had a substantial income."

Libby turned back to the rector. "You realised Liam was making a small fortune, and you failed to kill him on the first few tries, so you dreamed up your crazy scheme to kidnap Belinda and demand a ransom from Mike. You hoped the money would keep Liam off your back until you put your plan to kill him into operation. When the murder plan worked, you couldn't resist going ahead with the kidnapping."

The rector snickered. "No point wasting a good plan."

It was Max's turn to ask Belinda a question. "How did he trap you here?"

Belinda sank on the steps, hugging Sarah close. "He used my aunt's phone. She trusted him, of course. Who wouldn't trust the rector? He'd been worming his way into her life for months, visiting, pretending to help. He even talked to Mike and me about finding a suitable home for Aunt Antonia when the dementia got too bad. I was on my way to a shopping trip when I had a text from my aunt's phone, begging me to hurry over. I didn't even bother to let Mike know. I wasn't worried, as Aunt Antonia often panicked and sent for me, and it was usually because she couldn't work the TV, or she'd lost her reading glasses. When I arrived, he was here." She jerked her head towards the rector. "He made me coffee. Next thing I knew, I was locked in the stables."

Sarah, pale but composed, took up the tale. "He drugged you, Mum. Then he took your phone and used it to message me. The message said you'd been kidnapped, and I had to keep quiet and come over here. It said you wouldn't be harmed as long as I told nobody."

Tears sprang into Sarah's eyes. "I panicked. I should have said something to Robert, but I was too scared." Her shoulders shook. "I rang him. He's on his way, now, but I don't know how I'll face him. Will he ever forgive me?"

As he answered, Max's words beat a path to Libby's heart. "Of course, he'll forgive you. That's what being a couple is all about. You make mistakes, admit them, and forgive each other." Libby watched his kind, familiar face as he comforted Sarah, and her lips trembled. She had to swallow a sob, suddenly scared she was close to losing Max. She'd taken him for granted. Instead of telling him the truth, explaining her worries and fears about marriage, she'd pushed him away. She'd been cold and difficult towards him. What a fool she'd been. It would serve her right if he'd turned away to find comfort with the warm, sympathetic Kate Stephenson.

The look Max shot the rector would have frozen a stone. "I guess Mike wasn't paying up fast enough, so you thought you'd turn the screw." Libby recalled Mike's desperate expression. If only he'd told someone he was being blackmailed instead of keeping it to himself.

Max held up one hand. "I believe I can hear the police." He beamed cheerfully at the rector. "You'll be going away for a good, long time."

CHAPTER TWENTY TWO

Champagne

"At last, an evening to ourselves." Max put his feet up on his coffee table, a glass of wine in one hand. Bear lay across the floor while Shipley rolled happily in a patch of evening sunlight.

As she curled up in one of Max's oldest, most comfortable armchairs, Libby's stomach seemed to be tied in knots. She couldn't even touch the glass of New Zealand Pinot Noir. "Max, we need to talk." He stiffened, and Libby struggled to read the expression in his eyes as she confessed, "I saw a key, like Liam's, fall out of Kate Stephenson's bag."

She knew she was blushing, ashamed to have kept it from him, allowing jealousy of Kate Stephenson to interfere with their murder investigation. After the rector's arrest, a police search found gold keys and locked boxes, like Liam's, at the Papadopoulos couple's house. The pair had talked freely, desperate to distance themselves from Liam's murder. Apparently, all the conspirators had copies of Liam's passwords in identical boxes. The day Libby met the couple at Mike's farm, they'd been hoping to access his files on the farm computer.

"I didn't tell you about the key because…" she fiddled with a strand of her hair. "Because I wanted to solve the case myself." Her voice sounded very small. "I was jealous when you spent all evening talking to Kate at that horrible quiz."

Max looked surprised. "Jealous? But, I don't give a fig for Kate Stephenson. You told me you were worried about Mandy seeing her, so I kept an eye on her. We knew each other, years ago, so I used that as an excuse. You seemed to have your hands full." He hesitated. "To be honest, I was glad to talk to her about Debbie. I don't often get the chance to talk about my daughter with someone from the old days."

Libby's chest contracted. Max rarely referred to the guilt he felt over Debbie's riding accident. "Do you speak with Joe about his sister?"

He shook his head. "Not much. Don't really know how to start, after all these years. We're not good at these emotional things, Joe and I."

He gave a crooked grin and Libby's heart missed a beat. Max always seemed to be the strong one. So clever and capable; so sure of himself. He'd helped Libby through the bad times uncovering her husband's fraud, but tonight the man looked sad and vulnerable.

Maybe she'd taken Max's support for granted, not noticing that sometimes he needed her, too. She moved from the chair to sit beside him.

He took a deep breath. "Libby, I've been wondering. Are we making a mistake, going into business together? I think I might have talked you into it against your will, and it's seemed, lately, as though you're having second thoughts. I wish you'd tell me the truth. Would you be happier sticking with your cakes and chocolates?"

Libby took a moment to think. "This isn't about business, is it?"

"Not really."

She leaned closer, breathing in Max's familiar male smell. "I need to apologise—"

He turned to look into her eyes, and she put her finger against his lips. "No, I have to say this now. I've taken you for granted over the past couple of years. I've let my history with Trevor frighten me, and backed away whenever you mentioned marriage. I've been scared, you see. Going into business is one thing, but being a proper couple is another."

His face was very close as he murmured, "Do you want to be that? A proper couple?"

She smiled. "When I saw you with Kate

Stephenson, I was so jealous I could have scratched her eyes out, but it gave me the shock I needed. I can't expect you to wait any longer for me to decide what I want."

Max's eyes opened wider. He'd stopped breathing, and Libby knew their future now rested in her hands. Was she ready to commit, even if it meant giving up some independence and moving out of her beloved cottage?

It took less than a split second to decide. She slipped from the chair and knelt on the floor, her heart hammering against her ribs. "Max Ramshore, will you marry me?"

***

Libby could hardly wait for the next supper night with their friends.

"Everything's changing," Mandy grinned. "You two getting married, Reginald going back to America…"

"You better come visit, young lady," Reginald interrupted. "Bring that musician boyfriend."

Libby stared at Mandy and she blushed. "Didn't I mention? I went to London on the train, to see Steve. We're not exactly back together, but I'm going to see him again soon."

"And that," said Max, as he slid the cork from

a bottle of champagne, with only the gentlest of pops, "is worth another celebration."

Robert and Sarah, sitting so close Mandy had cackled and advised them to get a room, toasted each other. Robert said, "Sarah's never to leave my sight again without telling me where she's going."

Sarah and Libby exchanged a glance and Sarah winked. That state of affairs wasn't going to last long. Robert's new wife, none the worse for being drugged and locked up in an old stable full of mice and spiders, was tougher than she looked.

"By the way," Robert continued, "we're thinking of moving down to Somerset. Sarah's dad's handing over the running of the farm to Tim, and we're going to live nearby to lend a hand. I can work from anywhere and I fancy a taste of country life. It seems to have suited you, Mum."

Libby could hardly believe her luck. Life still had plenty of challenges: the new cafe in town was putting Frank's bakery in danger, and her semi-official role with the police could lead in many directions. Most of all, she missed her daughter Ali, far away on the other side of the world, but with Max at her side, she felt she could deal with anything that came her way. Robert living nearby would be the icing on the cake.

Joe and Claire were quiet, and Libby wondered if they felt side-lined by all the celebrations. She'd been planning to thank Claire for finding a new, trustworthy phobia therapist for Mandy. Kate Stephenson was under police investigation for the scam she'd used on Belinda, along with the Papadopoulos couple. Libby still shivered when she thought of Xavier and his wife. They might not have killed anyone, but they'd preyed mercilessly on vulnerable people across the world, making a small fortune from their heartless cons.

She cleared her throat, but before she could speak, Joe rose. "I want to make a toast." He stared at Libby through clear blue eyes. His smile was lopsided, like Max's. "Since you came to Exham, Mrs Forest, you've turned the place upside down. We were a quiet little backwater and you've transformed us all. Dad's been like a new man since you met, and I can't think of anyone I'd rather have in the family."

Max took Libby's hand as Joe raised his glass. "To my new stepmother."

Thank you for reading Murder at the Bridge. I hope you had fun with Libby, Max and the other inhabitants of Exham on Sea. If you enjoyed the story, please let other readers know, by adding a short review on Amazon.

Claim your FREE Exham on Sea Kitchen Cheat Sheet.

Libby Forest, the heroine of the Exham on Sea Mysteries, doesn't spend much time with her feet up. When she isn't hot on the trail of villains she's busy in the kitchen, seeking ways to make cooking easier and quicker.

The Exham on Sea Kitchen Cheat Sheet is a collection of her favourite tips and tricks in a handy pdf. It's exclusive to members of the Exham on Sea VIP Club and I'll send you a link to the Cheat Sheet as soon as you join.

As a cherished member of the VIP Club, you'll enjoy free books, short stories and fun bonuses, and early information on new books, sales and offers.

Claim your FREE Cheat Sheet at
www.francesevesham.com

Acknowledgements

I've had fun writing this, the fifth Exham on Sea mystery, but it takes more than an author to publish a book. A great many people have helped in the development of this book and I want to take the opportunity to say a really big thank you.

My 'Inner Circle' of readers and reviewers helped immeasurably with reading, revising and editing the book, as did Wendy Janes, my kind, efficient and knowledgeable editor.

I'm especially grateful to Nancy Dillow, Pippa Dunbar, Barbara Jensen, Alan Nixon, Pam Knox, Mary Robinson, Michelle Saunders, Susan Schuman, Robert Simon, Eileen Smith, and Frank Wright for their time, trouble, eagle eyes and kind support.

I do, however, claim any errors remaining in the story. They are entirely my own work.

Many readers have been kind enough to post reviews and comments on the Exham on Sea stories on Amazon, my website or their own blogs.

As ever, a big thank you goes to my husband. Dave provides the wonderful photographs gracing the covers of the Exham on Sea books, along with plenty of tea, sympathy and kind encouragement.

Finally, a word of caution about psychic scams. During my research I've been shocked to find how many exist, alongside plenty of other frauds designed to cheat people out of their hard-earned money. To me, psychic scams seem to be among the worst, because they're designed to frighten and prey on people who already feel vulnerable.

Please, please, never fall for one, either online or in the real world. If you live in the UK, you can report online scams by contacting Action Fraud www.actionfraud.police.uk/report_fraud at the National Fraud and Cyber Crime Reporting Centre, or by calling your local police.

The Exham on Sea Mysteries: Contemporary Cosy Crime Fiction
Murder at the Lighthouse 2015
Murder on the Levels 2016
Murder on the Tor 2016
Murder at the Cathedral 2017
Murder at the Bridge 2017

The Thatcham Hall Mysteries: Victorian Fiction
An Independent Woman 2014
Danger at Thatcham Hall 2015

48320796R00123

Printed in Poland
by Amazon Fulfillment
Poland Sp. z o.o., Wrocław